LIONESS

by

Brian Dorsey

LIONESS

Copyright © 2019 by Brian Dorsey

www.mountaineerwest.com

Chapter 1

Michelle Harper shuffled forward as the person in front of her in line took a step. The roar of conversations and other noises in the busy government building stabbed at her like a thousand needles. Inundated by the cacophony of the outside world, she slouched toward the floor and focused on the geometric shapes of the tiles at her feet.

Squares, circles, triangles … she calculated circumferences and angles to block the noise.

The pressure of a stranger's body brushing against hers caused her to jump.

"Sorry," grunted a short, bald man who squeezed between Michelle and the person behind her in the line.

Rattled, she quickly returned her gaze to the tiles — and the math — as the man disappeared into the swarming sea of bodies in the bustling main floor of Seattle-Tacoma metro-city federal service building.

A tap on her shoulder again startled her and she turned to see a frustrated woman standing behind.

"Move up," huffed the woman. "Don't leave a gap."

"Oh…yes. Sorry," replied Michelle, averting her gaze from the woman as she took another step forward. A crack in the tile now at her feet created a dozen new angles.

Too many. Too much.

Michelle looked up toward the massive ceiling, closed her eyes, and tried to calm her breathing. She wanted nothing more than to turn and run back to her apartment.

But she wouldn't. Not this time.

Her sister's voice, pleading her to not do what she was doing, echoed in Michelle's head as she opened her eyes. All she had to do was wait her turn, hand over the document, and everything would be better.

It had to be better.

This was the only way to fix things — to fix…herself.

But just the hover train ride across the Puget Sound from her apartment alone had exhausted and shaken her. Her mind was like a raw nerve.

Too many people … too many eyes on her.

The person in front of her stepped away and she took another step. The tile ended at the base of a raised platform. Michelle glanced up toward a large man in uniform at the reception desk of the Off-Earth Special Operations Service recruitment office.

"Next!" boomed the man, startling her. "Next!" he repeated.

She read the electronic nameplate at the front of the man's desk: Sergeant McCready, OE SOS Logistics.

"Can I help you?" he asked.

Michelle extended an old, faded document. "I'd like to talk to a recruit —"

"Speak up, please," said the sergeant.

"Um…yes," replied Michelle, her voice still barely above a whisper. "I'd like to see a recruitment officer, please."

The man took the document and examined it, then glanced down at Michelle. "This is for you?" he asked.

"Yes," she replied.

"Are you sure?"

"Um, yes. It was —"

"This is over a year old," said the sergeant. "And …" he paused, looking her over.

She involuntarily took a step back. His eyes scanning her body sent a shiver down her spine.

"… I'm sorry but this must have been a mistake to begin with," he continued. "OE SOS recruits are … well, not you."

"But I have the letter requesting that I —"

"I can only assume this was a clerical error," said the sergeant, trying not to laugh at the disheveled, meek creature standing in front of him. "And even if it wasn't a mistake, why didn't you come earlier? Why wait over a year?"

Michelle's head drifted back toward the floor. "Circumstances changed."

"Well, ma'am," replied the sergeant. "Even if this is legit, it's too old to speak directly with a recruiting officer. You'll need to file a request, which you can do via your wrist communicator, and then after it has been screened, you will get a notification to make an appointment with a recruitment officer."

"How long will that take?"

"That's not my department, ma'am," he replied.

"But I need to do this," said Michelle, tears welling up as she forced herself to take a step toward the man.

"And why is that?"

Her body tensed. She could feel herself start to shake as her breathing grew labored. "Because I…" She paused as her emotions began to overcome her.

The man shook his head, more out of pity than amusement by this point. "Look, miss. If you can't even say why you want to join a service that is going to send you off to Mars and beyond, fighting against our competitors, then how do you think you'll actually be able to do it."

"You don't understand," she begged. "I need to do this."

"Why?" he asked again.

"So I won't be like this anymore!" she shouted, her rage, fear, and frustration finally exploding from her core. "So I won't be fucking afraid to leave me apartment … to take a hover train … to talk …" She paused, suddenly feeling the eyes of dozens on her. "I'm sorry, I didn't —"

"Look, ma'am," said the sergeant, leaning forward.

Michelle again stepped backwards, away from him.

He quickly retreated, as if backing away from a startled animal, not wanting to upset her further. "Look, I think you have a lot of things you need to deal with before you think about becoming a soldier." He paused, sliding the document back across the desk to her. "Maybe you should just go."

Michelle took the document, squeezing it tightly in her hand.

"But…I…" She stopped, defeated and exhausted. Looking back toward the floor, she turned to walk away.

"Miss Harper!"

Michelle's heart jumped as she turned toward the source. "Um, yes?"

She looked up to see an exceptionally tall man in his mid-forties looking down at her. He had dark brown hair with the earliest hints of gray. He carried an air of confidence, bordering on arrogance, which instantly unsettled her.

"It's okay, Miss Harper," said the man. "I'm Lieutenant Colonel North. I'm an OE SOS doctor working in liaison with Consolidated Armaments Technologies Corporation."

"How do you know me?" asked Michelle, her anxiety continuing to grow. "I don't understand."

"Oh," replied North with a chuckle. "Your wrist device. When you, well anyone, enters a CAT or an OE SOS facility, your name is uploaded to our security data files."

"But why are you talking to me?"

"Because we've been waiting a long time for you, Miss Harper…or may I call you Michelle?"

"You have?" she asked, her head slowly rising to meet North's gaze. "Why?"

"When you turned down our offer to become an OE SOS officer last year, we'd hoped you would reconsider so we left your name on our list of potential recruits…so when you're name popped up as being in the recruiting facility, I came down right away to see if you'd changed your mind?"

"I have."

"Excellent," said North. "What caused the change of heart? I had assumed you would be finishing your doctorate studies."

Michelle felt her stomach start to churn but she took a deep breath. "I wasn't able to complete my studies because of…" She closed her eyes and exhaled heavily before opening them again. "I couldn't."

"No worry," replied North. "We can talk about that later."

"Sir," interjected the sergeant at the desk. "Does this mean you'd like me set up an appointment with a recruitment officer for her?"

"No," snapped North. "She doesn't need one." He looked back down toward Michelle. "She's already been accepted."

"Sir?" asked the sergeant.

"You can return to your duties, Sergeant," said North, his attention still on Michelle.

"Really?" Michelle's mouth curled into a smile, something she hadn't done in a long time.

"Of course," replied North. "The only question is when do you want to start?"

"Right now," shot back Michelle. "Today."

"I appreciate the enthusiasm," said North. "but I'm sure you'll need to wrap up some of your affairs, say some temporary goodbyes before training starts."

"I'm ready now," said Michelle.

"Won't you need to pack or gather some personal items?"

"I am assuming if I am an officer candidate, those things will be provided?"

"Yes, of course. But most new soldiers like to bring something with them that reminds them of home."

"No," replied Michelle. "I have to do this now."

"Hmm. If you're sure, then you can follow me to my office and sign the necessary documents. Then we can start discussing your training."

"Yes."

"Then follow me, Miss Harper, to your new future."

Michelle followed North toward an elevator behind the reception area.

As they moved past the sergeant at the desk, he glared at Michelle, who passively positioned herself on the opposite side of North.

The elevator opened and they stepped inside. "Don't worry about him," said North. "In no time at all, he'll be saluting you."

He leaned in a little closer as the elevator began to drift upward. "So why did you finally decide to take us up on our offer?"

"I...uh ..."

"We'll need to do a thorough review of your records, so you'll need to be completely up-front with us about everything from now on." He gave her a reassuring smile. "Honesty is one of our most important qualities here at OE SOS."

She felt the pressure inside her growing. "Because I never want to feel weak and afraid again," she replied, tears welling up in her eyes. She doubled over as a tornado of emotions swept through her body. "I can't do this anymore. I can't be this person."

North leaned back, smiling. "Well Michelle, we're in the business of helping those who want to become new people do just that." He placed his hand on her shoulder, leaning in again.

Michelle recoiled but recovered, somehow already feeling stronger. She even forced herself to look him in the eyes.

"And," continued North, "if you truly want to become a warrior, then one day you will fear nothing or no one."

She guffawed. "Yeah, right. That's impossible."

"It's possible, Michelle." He placed his other hand on her opposite shoulder. "Do you want to live the rest of your life as someone's prey…or as a predator?"

"I want to do whatever I have to in order to not feel like…me."

He released his grip on her, gently placing his hand on her head for a second. "Then we must talk about a new program I think you are perfect for, Michelle."

"What is it?"

"It is called the Consolidated Armaments Technologies Human Interface Soldier program…C.A.T.H.I.S. for short."

"CATHIS?" asked Michelle. "Sounds like an old woman's name."

North snickered. "Soon the entire planet will come to know the word CATHIS as the embodiment of power, speed, and strength. Just the name itself will strike fear in those that would take what is not theirs."

The elevator dinged at the 115th floor.

North stepped out of the elevator, turning toward Michelle.

"Now is the turning point, Michelle. Do you want to be a lamb for the rest of your life…or do you want to be a lion?" asked North.

Chapter 2

Everything faded away except the fleeing enemy.

The thick sulfuric smoke, the crack of gunfire, and the screams of the dying — they were nothing but echoes, distractions for Captain Cathis Harper as she ran across the field of waist-high yellow flowers.

The old her, when she was Michelle, would have gazed at the flowers for hours as they swayed in the gentle breeze, maybe even drawing them in her sketchbook. Now, she used their motion to calculate wind speed if a long-distance shot was needed.

But it wouldn't be.

Her target was moving at five miles per hour. Her average speed of twenty-five miles per hour would put her on target in seventeen seconds. It would be fifteen seconds if it wasn't for the round in her thigh. The nanocells were already at work, reducing the bleeding and blocking the pain receptors, but her speed was affected.

Ten seconds. The target was in pistol range but Cathis needed it to be up close, her orders were to leave a message.

She grabbed her knife from its sheath and pushed on. The target was tired, speed reducing. Three seconds. Two…

***

Cathis opened her eyes.

Sitting up in her bunk, the warm sensation of a tear rolling down her cheek gave her momentary pause before she wiped it away.

She rubbed her fingers together gently until the moisture was gone, trying to recall what she was dreaming about.

But she couldn't.

With a huff, she swung her legs off the bed.

The cold tile felt good against her feet as she took in the dimly lit, spartan stateroom. Her home for the last six months while onboard the cruiser OE SOS *Battle of Fallujah*, the room consisted of a small desk immediately in front of her bunk, her weapons and uniform lockers to her right, and gravity training module to the left.

The blinking green light from the flat screen on her desk told her a message was waiting.

"Lights," she said flatly, and the room grew slightly more luminous.

Cathis stood and moved to the desk.

"Kayla," she huffed, seeing the name of the sender. "Open message from Kayla Harper."

The screen flickered and the face of an attractive woman in her mid-twenties appeared. Thin and bubbly, Kayla's green eyes and dark hair were the only things that indicated her relation to Cathis.

The message began to play:

"Hey Cathis. Haven't heard from you in a few months so I thought I would...I dunno, say, hi." Kayla paused, clearly frustrated. "I know you're busy...but maybe you could find the time to send me a —"

"Close message," mouthed Cathis, ending her sister's message mid-sentence.

Cathis ran her hand over her face and exhaled heavily. She couldn't afford the distraction of her sister dumping guilt on her from over six hundred million kilometers away. Not when she had a mission coming.

Cathis stood and turned toward her locker.

Grabbing a black T-shirt, she pulled it over her back before selecting her tactical uniform.

Stepping into the uniform, she pressed the activation buttons on each wrist; the uniform tightened around her body. The reactive armor in her uniform gave off a slight *hum* as it activated. She then stepped into her boots and they too automatically adjusted for a perfect fit.

"Weapons locker open. Name: Harper, Captain, Off-Earth Special Operations Service. Codeword: Lioness."

The locker slid open and a quick smile came to her face.

Cathis took her tactical vest and secured it around her body. After attaching her sidearm holster to her leg, she took two pistols, one for the leg holster and one for her vest, and slid them into place.

Pausing, she placed her hand to her jaw and rubbed it slightly as she chose her primary weapon. She had two choices. First was the CAT M-43 assault rifle. It utilized the latest CAT technology in kinetic energy multiplication, giving it a 100-round magazine capacity with 50 armor-piercing and 50 antipersonnel rounds, selected by a button behind the trigger guard. The other weapon was the CAT M-7 assault shotgun. Aside from advances in propellant charges that reduced shell size to increase capacity to twenty rounds per magazine and overall weight reduction, it was the basically the same weapon one of her Marine ancestors would have used over two hundred years earlier during the battle for which her ship was named.

But it was big, loud, and terrifying. Exactly what this mission called for…

Cathis let out a satisfied grunt as she placed her hands around the shotgun. Locking the weapon's lanyard into place on her vest, she filled her pouches with magazines…260 rounds for the shotgun and 200 for the pistols would do.

Finally, she removed her helmet from the locker and held it in her right hand.

"Secure locker."

The locker latched shut as she turned and exited her stateroom.

"Lights," she said as the door closed and the room went black.

***

Walking down the passageway, Cathis was joined by the ship's Commanding Officer, Jalyn Zhang. Zhang, tall and of Chinese descent, walked with the confidence typical of an OE SOS fleet commander.

"Good morning, Captain Harper," said Zhang. "Ready to go hunting?"

"Always," replied Cathis. "Are you joining us for the briefing, Commander?"

"Yes. Backus will cover the details, but I thought I'd observe."

"Your prerogative, Commander," said Cathis. "Any sign of Cal or RSR ships?"

"None," replied Zhang. "The Restored Soviet Republic is staying clear since we authorized unrestricted attacks on Caliphate facilities after the attack off Mars. I'm guessing they're hoping we'll wear each other down, making it easier for them to move in to the area afterwards."

"And the Cals?"

"They're mostly tied up trying to consolidate forces closer to Mars and their nearby stations, so I don't expect anything more than a scout ship or maybe a frigate, if anything. Nothing we can't handle."

"As long as you keep my dropships' six clear, that's all I care about."

"My orders are to do just that," replied Zhang. He paused briefly. "I wonder how willing everyone would be to fight if we still handled our beefs back on Earth?"

Cathis slowed, turning toward Zhang. "Accords or not, you just point my team towards a Cal or RSR force and we'll take 'em out…that's what I was made for."

Zhang's mouth curled in a moment of reflection about Cathis statement. "I guess you were," he said. "But I think everyone's much happier with you and your kind doing what you're 'made for' far from Earth."

Cathis knew he wasn't talking about her elite OE SOS assault force but her specifically — and the few other enhanced soldiers in the C.A.T.H.I.S. program. "Don't know if happier is the right word," said Cathis.

"Safer perhaps is better," posited Zhang.

"Hmm," replied Cathis. It was no secret most people on Earth felt modified soldiers such as herself were just one step away from mindless killing machines. But they sure didn't mind her and others like her fighting and dying in the darkness of space. "Safer…let's go with that."

Cathis stopped as they reached the door to the briefing room. "You first, Commander."

Zhang entered the room to 'attention on deck'.

"At ease," said Zhang, taking position beside his Tactical Officer, Lieutenant Commander Amanda Backus. Backus was of average height and was lean, but not skinny. She kept her red hair tied into a tight bun, always within regulations. Cathis liked Backus; she'd never get in the mud and blood like one of her team, but she knew her job. If any Cal ships did show up, Cathis was confident Backus and *Battle of Fallujah*'s guns would handle them.

Also in the room were Cathis' three lieutenants: Yang, Morris, and Carson. Lieutenant Charles Yang, a powerful-looking man with a tight crew-cut and a permanent stern look, was closely examining the map. Yang was her senior platoon commander and had himself been selected for the C.A.T.H.I.S. program, but a seemingly insignificant genetic mutation had disqualified him. Lieutenant Cassidy Morris, tall and lean with brown hair tied into a tight bun, stood almost at attention. Lieutenant Manny Carson, an African-American with his head shaved bald, was laser-focused on Cathis.

Cathis stepped past Zhang and Backus, stopping in front of the large 3-D digital map of the Caliphate mining facility on asteroid Delta-3 in the Hilda asteroid belt.

"We're a go for 0800 ZULU," said Cathis, scanning the faces of her lieutenants. "Deep space scans are currently clear so it looks like it will be a smooth ride until their air defense systems pick us up."

Backus stepped forward. "Once their air defense systems illuminate the dropships, we'll be able to target them from close orbit."

Cathis then turned toward First Platoon's commander. "Carson," she continued as a section of the map flashed red, "First Platoon will dress out in full power gear and atmo-suits." She pointed to the map. "You'll insert here, here, and here. You will take out their anti-air batteries and keep as much of their security forces tied down as possible. Once you're on the ground make sure you ping *Fallujah* and confirm your locations are detected by their guns so they don't nail you with any kinetic rounds from orbit."

"Yes, Captain," replied Carson.

"Yang, Second Platoon will do a direct breach of the facility at the following locations," said Cathis, pointing out the insertion points. "Your main objectives will be the communications center and the armory."

"Captain," said Yang, with a nod that confirmed she understood.

"Third Platoon. First Sergeant and I will be with you."

"Yes, Captain," replied Morris.

"We'll direct breach the southern and eastern sections then clear the loading docks, engineering, and living quarters." Cathis turned toward a tall man in the shadows of the room. "First Sergeant?"

First Sergeant Greeves stepped into the light. Greeves was in his late thirties with dark hair that was cut high and close and a thick beard that challenged, but did not break, regulations. Greeves had been with Cathis since the beginning. Before that, he had worked with Earth-bound Special Projects, but the details of his history were sketchy even for elite OE SOS units such as hers.

"This facility is older than most," said Greeves, his deep, slow voice commanding attention, "so nothing above frag grenades. If we punch a hole in their containment, we'll be sucking on vacuum … that also means no spraying the fucking walls with rounds if you don't need to. Shoot with purpose and hit what you're shooting at."

Cathis stepped in front of Greeves.

"You may have heard we're here to track new sources of titanium, but we all know this mission is payback for the attack on our hospital ship *Holland* off Mars." She paused, taking the time to lock eyes with each of her officer before continuing. "Every time a Cal falls in your sights, remember our brothers and sisters who died suffocating in the dark."

Cathis snaps to attention.

"What's the key to victory?!"

"Speed and violence," shouted Yang, Morris, and Carson in unison.

Cathis nodded in approval before turning toward Morris.

"Lieutenant Morris, you have two new guys. Are they ready?"

"Lane and Donald. They both scored well in basic and in Advanced Space Combat School."

"None of that means shit the first time a bullet whizzes past their heads," added Greeves. "But Sergeant Acree will be right on their asses the whole time."

"This should be a good first mission for them, Captain," said Morris. "The whole service wants payback."

"And we'll be the ones to get it," added Cathis with a smile. "Won't we, Lieutenant?"

"Yes, ma'am!" shouted Morris.

"Get your teams ready," ordered Cathis and the lieutenants dispersed to prepare for the attack.

"Your team looks ready," said Backus as the lieutenants left the room.

"They are," replied Cathis.

Backus' jaw clinched in anger. "Fleet troops died on *Holland* too, including my cousin," she said through gritted teeth. "I want you to make them pay."

Cathis smiled. "Consider me your avenging angel of death," replied Cathis. "Just keep our heads covered and we'll send 'em all to hell."

Backus acknowledged with a nod. "We'll do our job too, Captain," said Backus. "If it were up to me, we'd turn that whole facility to ash from orbit."

Backus' eyes tightened with rage. "Make it hurt," said Backus before exiting the briefing room.

"Anything else you need from fleet?" asked Zhang.

"Just don't let your Tactical Officer get too crazy with those kinetic rounds," replied Cathis as she watched Backus exit the compartment. "Just hit the sites that illuminate our dropships and any targets we call in once we're on the deck. We'll want to get any data we can on mining operations and titanium resources they may have found in the area."

Zhang laughed. "So it *is* about titanium and not revenge?"

Cathis smiled. "It's about both."

Zhang nodded in acknowledgement. "I'll be on the bridge when you launch, but all comms will go through Backus in CIC." Zhang turned and made toward the exit but stopped just before leaving. "I'll make sure she stays on mission."

Cathis felt Greeves' hand on her shoulder.

"You good, Captain?" asked Greeves. "Not having any more issues with that tear thing?"

"Five by five, First Sergeant," she replied, lying. "Hasn't happened lately."

"Good," said Greeves. "It's nothing to worry about anyway. I've seen it with other C.A.T.H.I.S. Just some weird brain-computer interface issue you guys have sometimes, I guess. It seems to pop up after a few years but goes away pretty quickly." Greeves positioned himself squarely in front of Cathis. "You'd tell me if it was a problem wouldn't you, Captain?"

"You don't have to worry about me, First Sergeant. You should know that by now."

"Yes, ma'am," he said with a smile. "I've been with you since you were a butter bar and you are one of the best…but it's my job as First Sergeant to ask."

"Well, I'm fine," she replied.

"Excellent," he declared. "You ready to go be lions?"

"Damn straight," she replied. "Let's go get us some lambs."

***

Cathis walked along the four rows of soldiers as they prepared their stations onboard their dropship prior to detachment from *Fallujah*.

She watched as each soldier went through the normal procedure.

First, since only Carson's platoon would be dressed out in atmo-suits, they tested their helmets and the forced air backup that would provide thirty minutes of air if compartment integrity was lost. Next was a second validation of gear to back up the one performed in the hangar bay prior to embarking. Finally, each sergeant verified their squad was properly secured into their harnesses.

After the appropriate amount of time for them to complete their tasks, Cathis turned to Greeves and gave him a nod.

"Report by chalks!" boomed Greeves.

"Chalk One ready!" reported Sergeant Acree.

"Chalk Two ready!" reported Lieutenant Morris.

"Chalk Three ready!" reported Staff Sergeant Morgan.

"Chalk Four ready!" reported Sergeant Xu.

"ALL UNITS STAND BY FOR RELEASE IN THREE MINUTES," came a warning across the dropship's intercom.

Cathis stopped in front of Private Lane and gave him a stern look. "You ready to take the fight to the enemy, Private?"

"Yes, ma'am!" shouted Lane, his muffled shout still audible through his helmet.

The soldier beside Lane, Corporal Nash, slapped Lane's helmet playful. "Don't worry, Captain. Lane here's ready for his cherry blast."

"I'm ready, Captain," said Lane.

Cathis knew he was trying to convince himself just as much as he was her.

"Just remember your training and forget everything else when you hit the deck," said Cathis. She leaned in close. "And it's real simple…see a Cal, shoot a Cal."

"TWO MUNITES TO RELEASE."

Cathis moved to her position and strapped herself into her harness. Just before she slid her helmet over her head, she looked toward Greeves, who was in position adjacent to her. "All Ravens report status."

She listened as each of the ten dropships, holding thirty OE SOS soldiers each, reported they were ready.

"Bravo Foxtrot, this is Alpha. All Raven standing by for release," she reported to *Fallujah's* CIC.

"ROGER, ALPHA. STAND BY FOR RELEASE IN THREE-ZERO SECONDS."

Cathis took a deep breath. After the last month onboard *Fallujah*, it would be good to step foot on a something with real gravity. And to shoot something other than holographic targets.

"TEN…NINE…"

A flash of a memory shot through Cathis' mind. It was the yellow field of flowers again.

But it faded as quickly as it appeared. She looked across toward Greeves.

"You good?" came across their personal circuit.

"Fine," she replied.

"THREE…TWO…ONE…"

The metallic *clang* of the magnetic mooring arms releasing told Cathis they were free of the cruiser. Next, the dropship reoriented to align with the others for initial boost, leaving the chalks leaning at a 30-degree angle.

"Alpha, this is Bravo Foxtrot. All Raven's indicate good release. Transferring tactical control to Alpha."

"Roger, Bravo Foxtrot," replied Cathis, taking command of the dropships. Cathis closed her eyes, accessing the dropship positions via her internal interface. "Stand by for boost on my mark…mark!"

The rattle and hum of the dropship's booster carried through the metallic frame as the attack formation accelerated toward Delta-3.

"Initiate deceleration and landing protocol," she ordered to the dropship pilots.

Cathis was focused on visualizing the breach as the dropship began to shake as a result of deceleration. She'd already memorized what schematics were available for the facility and she walked through each corridor mentally.

The dropship shuddered as it blasted through the rudimentary terraforming barrier and Cathis looked over her troops.

With the exception of Lane and Donald, the rest of her team were all veterans of the dirty, violent war fought between the Restored Soviet Union, the Caliphate, and the Sino-American Cooperative. Although Earth's leaders said that human-kind had evolved beyond spilling blood between nations on their home planet, they seemed to have no problem spilling across the rest of the Solar System.

But politics where of no concern to her. Her responsibility was the mission.

Soon the volume of communications cracking over the dropship's intercom increased, telling her they were close. The *tick-tick-tick* of ice particles hitting the hull was replaced with the *rattling* of shrapnel echoing through the dropship's hull as anti-aircraft rounds exploded near them.

"Alpha, this is Bravo Foxtrot. Ground targets designated as Bunker One through Seven," cracked Backus' voice over the fleet circuit patched into Cathis' helmet. "Batteries release from mounts one-one, two-one, five-one, seven-one, and nine-one. Kinetic rods inbound."

But as *Fallujah*'s ordnance made their way toward their targets, the Caliphate air-defenses fired their last rounds. A metallic screech echoed through the dropship as a round exploded against the hull, sending shards of metal flying through the troop compartment.

Cathis let out a grunt as her body was slammed into the harness holding her in place.

A puff of air caused her ears to pop. Her helmet pressurized and her skin rippled as it first began to freeze and then warm when the tactical suit's heating elements activated.

"Sergeant!" shouted Private Lane.

Cathis looked toward Sergeant Acree. A shard of metal had ripped through him. In the limited gravity of the damaged dropship, the blood oozing from Acree's open chest coalesced around his open chest cavity and slowly broke away into small bubbles.

Scanning the compartment, she saw two other soldiers had been killed.

As capsules of the dead men's blood floated through the cabin, Cathis focused her gaze on Lane, then toward Lieutenant Morris. Even though Morris couldn't see Cathis' face through her helmet, she held the gaze long enough for Morris to understand.

"Keep your shit together, Lane," barked Morris over the cacophony.

Lane gave a nod, his face visible through standard infantry visor, devoid of color.

"STANDBY!" cracked over the intercom.

"Steady!" ordered Cathis as the dropship slammed to a stop. The bubbles of blood slowly drifting downward hit the deck with a splash. "Ready for breach!"

Cathis looked down toward the hatch at her feet as the shriek of metal being cut by the dropships breaching laser rang in her ears.

She felt her heart rate increase — from 50 to 53 according to her interface data — in anticipation of what was coming.

The metallic screech stopped, and Cathis grunted through the pressure shift, as the dropship's status light shifted from red to green.

"Release harnesses!" she ordered as the breaching hatch slid open and she leapt into the opening.

Cathis hit the deck, immediately raising her weapon and firing a blast of metal pellets into a Caliphate soldier. Corporal Nash landed behind her but his head snapped backward as a round tore into his helmet. Shifting her aim, she fired, and the second enemy soldier toppled over. "Move!" she yelled, rushing forward, her troops following behind.

Cathis moved quickly. Sweeping the firing lane in front of her; one Caliphate soldier after another fell.

Coming to a large industrial door, she took up position against the wall to its right, looking across toward Greeves on the left of the door. "Make entry."

"Access the door," said Greeves to the two soldiers behind him.

Two soldiers ran up to the door and attached a shaped charge in the center before rushing back into position.

"All units report!" barked Cathis into her helmet comms.

"Second Platoon on deck. Moving toward objective. Three casualties."

"First Platoon on deck. First Squad lost on landing. Establishing perimeter outside of the containment. One casualty due to failed atmo suit."

"Roger," replied Cathis before allowing her neuro-interface to activate the fleet comms circuit. "Bravo Foxtrot, this is Alpha. All units on the deck, moving toward objectives."

Cathis turned back toward First Sergeant and gave a nod. "Breaching!"

Cathis exhaled heavily as the pressure wave from the blast washed over her and she pivoted to enter the massive hole created by the blast.

Rushing into the engineering room with First Sergeant at her side, she felt the sting of a round tearing into her shoulder.

Letting out a grunt, she centered her sights on the enemy in front of her and fired. The enemy soldier disappeared in the flash of her muzzle.

"You okay?" asked First Sergeant.

Three men in technician coveralls burst from behind a large container for an exit on the far end of the room.

Cathis leaned spun toward them. She leaned forward, peering down her sights as she methodically put a round into each man.

She turned back toward Greeves. The pain in her shoulder faded as the neuro-blockers embedded in her body took effect and she registered the interface data update that nanocells were already encasing the round in her shoulder. Ninety-three percent combat capable according to the interface. "Morris, hook up the data link," ignoring Greeves' question. "Once you've hacked their controls, pass the data to *Fallujah*."

She turned back to Greeves. "Let's go."

Moving forward, Cathis led the way as they made their way through engineering to the next compartment.

An old wooden door was in place for privacy, and of no structural or tactical importance, so she sent it flying open with a powerful kick.

She stepped inside and pivoted to her right when a Cal soldier grabbed at her weapon. The soldier pushed hard against the barrel of her shotgun but was not strong enough, as Cathis grabbed his head with her left hand and slammed it into the wall before tossing him halfway across the room. The crack of Greeves' rifle told her he had finished the job and she continued forward.

"Second squad should be in the passage adjacent to us," reported Greeves as they reached the hardened door at the opposite side of the room.

"Alpha, this is Bravo Foxtrot. We've successfully accessed ground facility controls remotely. Standing by to default all internal access doors to open,' came Backus' voice from *Fallujah*.

"Roger, Alpha," replied Cathis. "Open all internal doors."

"Activating in three…two…one …"

The massive door in front of them slid open and Cathis sent the surprised Cal soldier flying into the wall of the passageway with a blast from her shotgun.

Cathis stepped into the passage and moved forward quickly to the next opening.

Turning a corner, she saw Privates Lane and Donald taking cover behind an open entrance to storage compartment.

"Why aren't you moving forward, Privates?"

Private Donald looked up at Cathis as she stood over him. "Captain, there are three Cal soldiers inside, but they are with a group of civilians."

Cathis stared blankly at Donald then turned toward Lane. "Clear the room, Privates."

"But…the civilians?" posed Lane.

Casting a disappointed glance toward Greeves, Cathis leaned over and snatched a grenade from Lane's vest. She looked up to Greeves.

He had one of his grenades in his hand.

Both activated their grenades and tossed them into room.

Cathis stood over Lane and Donald as they curled their bodies in anticipation of the blast. Tightening her body, she remained erect while the grenades detonated, sending debris and smoke flying through the opening. "Return to your squad," directed Cathis to the two green privates.

As Lane and Donald scurried back to their team, Greeves and Cathis entered the storage compartment.

Looking down the length of her barrel, Cathis scanned the carnage she and Greeves had caused. The Caliphate soldiers were dead, almost unrecognizable as humans, as they had clearly tried to shield the civilians from the blast.

But they had failed. The others were dead or dying except for a man in his twenties.

The man, his left leg mangled and blood oozing from multiple wounds to his torso, slowly raised his hand.

A burst from Greeves' rifled knocked him back to the floor.

"Clear right!" yelled Greeves.

"Clear left!" answered Cathis as they both came to a stop near the opposite wall.

A closed manual door on the opposite wall drew Cathis' attention and she moved toward it, with Greeves beside her.

After a preparatory glance toward Greeves, Cathis fired a round into each hinge and kicked it open.

Light flooded the small room, and an old man on his knees with his hands in the air came into view.

Her interface translated his Arabic as he spoke.

"Please! I am not a soldier …"

As he spoke, Cathis felt herself begin to drift.

"…I am not a solider, I —"

The man's head disappeared in a mist of red as Cathis refocused and fired her weapon.

"You sure you're okay?" asked Greeves.

"I'm fine. Let's get back —"

Chapter 3

Cathis opened her eyes, immediately closing them against the bright overhead light.

Opening them again, she saw a man leaning over her prone body.

"Wait!" he pleaded as she grabbed his wrist. "You're safe."

As Cathis regained her senses, and data from her interface began to flow, she recognized the man, in his thirties with a military haircut, was wearing a medical uniform and an OE SOS security badge.

But she did not recognize the room.

And it definitely wasn't a medical bay of a ship.

"Where am I?"

"You're back on Earth," answered the man. "My name is Michael. I'm a medical technician and this is a CAT medical facility … you're home, Captain Harper."

"What happened?"

"A round penetrated your helmet on your last mission."

"Last mission?" She struggled to recall what had happened. She knew they were in the Hilda belt…she closed her eyes, trying to force the memory to her conscious.

"You were in an induced coma," said the man. "They may have already downloaded the mission so you might be a bit fuzzy. Either way, I don't have the clearance to know —"

"How long have I been out?" interrupted Cathis.

"I don't know, Captain. But you have been here for two weeks."

Cathis' attention was drawn to a tall man in his fifties with salt-and-pepper hair entering the room.

Finally, a familiar face.

"Colonel North," said Cathis.

"Well, that should about do it," said Michael, standing and starting toward the exit.

"Captain Harper," answered North before pausing to cast an inquisitive glance toward Michael.

"Updating charts for the next shift, Colonel," offered Michael.

North gave the man a dismissive nod before turning toward Cathis again. "How are you, Captain?"

"I don't know, Colonel," replied Cathis. "Shouldn't you be telling me?"

"Well," said North as he sat on the stool next to her bed. "You let yourself get shot in the head."

"Sorry to inconvenience you," quipped Cathis.

"It *was* an inconvenience," retorted North. "And an expensive one at that." North continued, flipping through screens on a medical tablet. "Even though the helmet slowed the projectile, it still did significant damage to both your backup interface processor and your occipital lobe."

Cathis let her hand drift to the back of her head. Her fingers ran over the rough bump of a scar where part of her hair had been shaved.

"Just another scar to add to your collection," said North. "But your down time did allow us to upgrade your visual suite."

Cathis' hand slid from her head. "Upgrade?" she said with a smile. "Did you give me x-ray vision or something?"

"No," chuckled North, but we have a new rod and cone enhancement protocol we are trying that should give 10/10 vision and increase your night vision clarity by fifteen percent."

"No shit?"

"Anyway," continue North in a tone that reminded Cathis he was much more pretentious than humorous. "We also used muscle stimulation and bone densification therapy to keep you in fighting shape while your brain healed … well, at least eighty-seven percent of top shape.”

“So that means I’m ready to get back to my unit?” she asked. Earth held nothing for her.

“Almost. We have one more procedure to validate your new secondary chip and run a simulated mission download. You’ll need to be conscious for us to run the final tests…and to reset your baseline.”

“When?”

“Tomorrow.”

“Good. I need to get back out there.”

North placed his hand on her shoulder. “What you need right now, Captain, is to get some rest. You know that C.A.T.H.I.S. troops only make up one percent of OE SOS forces, so you’re kind of valuable…financially and tactically speaking.”

“I didn’t think you recruited me for my personality, Colonel,” replied Cathis.

“No, we didn’t,” said North flatly. “Now get some rest.”

***

Asleep in the dark medical room, Cathis’ muscles twitched as she dreamed.

She was running in the field of yellow flowers again.

The sound of her rhythmic breathing and the pounding of her feet seemed intensified as she bore down on her target; she was close …

The image of a woman and child exploded inside her brain —

Cathis jerked awake.

Exhaling heavily, she wiped a tear from her cheek before reaching to feel the scar on the back of her head.

She remembered the images. The flowers … and the woman and child. But nothing else.

Was this the same fragment of a dream that had haunted her for the last seven standard months? She closed her eyes, trying to recall more.

Nothing.

Falling back into the bed, she stared blankly at the ceiling.

***

Cathis ran her hand down the sleeve of her uniform as she waited for the final test that would allow her to return to combat.

Movement at the entrance drew her attention.

"Greeves?" she asked, surprised to see her First Sergeant standing in front of her. "What are you doing here?"

"What?" he replied playfully. "I can't visit my injured Company Commander?"

"No. I mean what are you doing on Earth?"

"I just do what I'm told, Captain," replied Greeves. "Looks like the brass was happy with our last mission so they gave the company some leave…and sent me back here to support an inspection of ASCS."

"The mission?" She still couldn't remember. "What happened?"

"We won…and you got shot."

"No shit. What happened?"

"This might be fucked up, Captain, but if you don't remember, I'm not allowed to tell you."

"Jesus, Greeves, not the mission. What happened to me?"

"After Lane and Donald — they've been transferred back to an Earth-bound unit by the way — failed to clear a room. You and I went in …there must have been a Cal soldier hiding under one of the bodies, or he came in from another passage. He got behind us…"

"We missed one? No."

"No one's perfect…even you." He paused. "And it has happened before…"

"That was a long time ago," she replied.

"But both times you hesitated before it —"

"What? There's no way I hesitated." She sat back on the examination table, trying to recall the moments before she was shot.

"Are you sure you're okay?" asked Greeves. "This is the time to tell the docs anything that's been bothering you…you know, while already in the shop for repairs."

"I'm fine." Cathis stood again, brushing her sleeve one more time. "And after today I'll be ready to get back out there."

"That's all I needed to hear, Captain," replied Greeves.

Cathis heard the tapping of the medical technician's heels on the tile thirty seconds before the woman entered the room and let out a quick chuckle. Heels on a soldier. Only on Earth.

The woman entered the room, stopping just inside. "Hello, Captain," said the woman with a forced smile. "I'm Corporal Meade and I'll be running your diagnostics this morning."

"Well, hello, Corporal Meade," said Greeves, looking her over.

Meade responded with a smile. "And you are?"

"Just leaving," replied Greeves as he turned and moved toward the exit. "Your team will be ready when you are, Captain," he said to Cathis before leaving.

"He must not be too bad to work with," said Meade. Meade was attractive, blonde, and perky — just the way Colonel North liked his technicians. Cathis noticed the loose bun in which the tech's hair was tied with several stray hairs falling out. She also noticed the slightly wrinkled uniform and non-regulation earrings.

"Let's get on with it, Corporal," said Cathis. Every second she looked at the girl playing soldier made Cathis want to get back to her kind even more.

"Yes. Of course." The tech slid a small device into a tiny port just behind Cathis' right ear. "We'll do the subconscious download first then run the diagnostics to validate that recall protocols are effective."

Cathis' thoughts drifted back to her conversation with Greeves. Had she hesitated?

"Captain?"

Meade's voice refocused her.

"Just do whatever you need to do so I can get a thumbs up from Colonel North," huffed Cathis. "I'm ready to…" She paused, losing consciousness.

Cathis opened her eyes as a tear rolled down her cheek. Wiping the tear away, she turned toward the technician. She heard a harsh beeping from the tablet as the technician reviewed the data.

"What did you see, Captain?" asked the tech, focused on the tablet.

"What do you mean?"

"We uploaded a simulated mission so you should have flashes of that simulation. Your neuro readout shows REM activity so there was something. Let me pull up what you were dreaming about and I'll see what the problem is." A few flicks of her finger and the tech began to watch the visual representation of what had run through Cathis' subconscious. "Okay, we have good video so we…"

The technician paused, her eyes widening.

"What is it?" asked Cathis as the woman continued to focus on the screen.

Cathis furrowed her brow when the tech let out a gasp, placing her hand to her mouth.

"What is it?" demanded Cathis.

The technician was visibly shaking, unresponsive.

"Corporal!"

The boom of Cathis' voice startled the tech and she finally turned toward her but wouldn't make eye contact.

"What did you see?" asked Cathis slowly.

"I…uh…" stammered the technician.

"Was it the rape?"

"What? No. I —"

"That will be enough, Corporal," echoed North's voice as he entered the room. "I'll take it from here."

"Uh…yes, Colonel," replied the technician, almost leaping from her stool to hand North the tablet.

North took the tablet and gave the technician a reassuring smile. "Please wait in my office so we can debrief you on what you saw."

"Yes," said the technician, giving Cathis a quick, frightened glance before scurrying out of the room.

"Good morning, Captain," said North.

"What's wrong, Colonel?"

"Nothing. Corporal Meade just probably made an error in setting up the simulation."

"Your tech saw something," said Cathis.

"I wouldn't worry about it. Just let me reset the simulation and try again."

Cathis saw a bead of sweat run down North's forehead. North didn't sweat.

"Are you sure—"

***

North hit enter on the showdown tab of his tablet and Cathis fell back into the examination bed, unconscious.

North let out a heavy sigh as two guards took up position at the entrance.

"Shit," he cursed as he reviewed the video. At least it seemed that Cathis hadn't had any conscious recall. She could be reset and retested. But the technician would have to be dealt with. "Damn it," he grumbled, realizing that he would have one less piece of eye candy in his office.

He looked over Cathis as she lay on the table. She *had* been the perfect candidate for the program.

But then she refused them.

Hopefully, the version of her that eventually begged him to become a soldier hadn't been too broken.

She couldn't be. He had invested too much time and a huge chunk of his reputation and standing on her and the others like her.

"Get ready," he said to the two guards as his hands moved over the tablet, resetting the event — and Cathis' memory of it.

His hand paused over the ACTIVATE tab and he looked toward the guards. "If you have to act, aim for the head."

***

Cathis opened her eyes.

"Colonel?" she asked. "I thought a tech would be running the diagnostic?"

"They started but had problems, so we stopped the test," replied North, waiving for the guards to stand down.

"Problems?"

"On our end, Captain. No concern for you."

"Why don't I remember the tech coming in?"

"You've done this enough," replied North with a chuckle. "You know there can be short term memory lapses after a procedure … and you know it should come back soon."

"Yes," said Cathis, placated. "When can we go again?"

"We're going to need to upload our software again and run some stand-alone testing so not until tomorrow."

"Tomorrow?" grunted Cathis. "What the hell am I supposed to do here until then?"

"You could visit your sister," offered North. "She has contacted OE SOS several times after learning you were injured."

Cathis exhaled heavily. She cared for her sister, but it seemed like after Cathis had joined the program, their talks always ended with Kayla sad.

But it was probably better than sitting in the hospital all day.

"Fine," said Cathis, hopping down from the examination table.

"Good," replied North. "0800 tomorrow and we'll get you back out there."

"I'll be here," said Cathis, walking past the guards and heading toward the door.

***

After Cathis exited, North motioned for the guards to leave.

Turning toward a screen on the table behind him, North let out a heavy sigh. He tapped on the keyboard and the image of a middle-aged Chinese man in a suit flashed onto the screen.

"Mr. Dzu," said North. "I am assuming you were notified of the anomaly."

The man stared at North, expressionless. "What is her status?"

"She is stable. One of the…events was still detectable in her subconscious memory."

"Which mission?" Dzu's face tightened.

"The farmhouse," replied North but quickly continued. "But she's been reset and we'll be able to fully assess her tomorrow. I just need to add another algorithm to ensure she's cleared."

"And if she can't be cleared?" asked Dzu, leaning in toward the screen.

"Normal protocol will be followed."

"See that it is, doctor," replied Dzu. "Where is she now?"

"She's visiting her sister."

"You let her leave the facility?"

"Yes," replied North. "If she sat here all night, she would be thinking about this place and could possibly recall the tech's response when they saw the memory and that could spark a flashback. If she's with her sister, she will be too frustrated to think about the technician…and we have assets in place near the sister as well."

"Very well," huffed Dzu. "What are you doing about the technician?" asked Dzu.

"The normal protocol, as well," said North.

"You know how damaging it could be if one of your toys malfunctions in any sort of public forum here on Earth?"

"You don't have to remind me —"

The screen closed.

"Shit," cursed North under his breath.

Corporal Meade waited anxiously outside Colonel North's office. The images from Cathis' memory stabbed at her senses as she paced back in forth. Her stomach tightened and she doubled over, trying to take in more air to calm herself. As she struggled to force the images from her mind, she didn't see North approaching.

"Are you okay, Corporal?" asked North.

"Oh, Colonel," she replied, still trying to catch her breath. "I didn't —"

"I'm sure you have a lot of questions," interrupted North as he activated the door to his office. "Come inside and we'll get everything squared away."

Meade squeezed past North, who'd taken up part of the entrance so she would have to make contact with him to enter, and stopped in front of his desk.

"Please. Sit," said North, walking behind his desk to sit.

***

North looked across his desk at Corporal Meade. She sat up erect, but glanced around the room nervously, her first clinched tight.

"So," he began. "I reviewed the files from the diagnostic you ran on Captain Harper. I just need to know what you saw."

"It was horrible," replied Meade, her face pale. "It didn't make any sense. The soldiers were —"

North raised his hand to silence her. "It's okay," he said with a reassuring smile. "What you saw was an incoherent jumble of memories, nightmares…noise that happens sometimes with our more experienced C.A.T.H.I.S. They see a lot and as the downloads and upgrades accumulate, it sometimes starts getting all mixed together in their subconscious."

"So it wasn't real?"

"No," replied North. "What you saw was her subconscious trying to piece together a story out of a hundred different memories and thoughts." He let out sigh, feigning pity for Cathis. "Unfortunately, with the things they do see, their minds tend to weave together some pretty good nightmares … but that's all that they are, Corporal Meade."

Meade looked toward the floor and exhaled, releasing some of her anxiety. "Good, because…"

She paused, looking back up to North. "But what she did to them … did she actually do that?"

"Like I said, Corporal, you were watching a nightmare, not a memory."

North glanced over Meade's shoulder as a man entered the room. He was tall, with a bald head and a perfectly fitted uniform. "Captain

Burns, come in," he said as the man situated himself next to Meade.

Meade glanced up toward Burns. "I'm sorry, sir. I didn't mean to keep you from another —"

"It's fine, Corporal," replied North. "Captain Burns is here for you."

"Sir?" Meade glanced up toward Burns.

"I know it's been a stressful day so I'm giving you the rest of the day off. Captain Burns and Lieutenant Miles will make sure you get home safely."

Meade turned to see another man, tall and muscled with sandy hair, enter North's office.

"I'm okay, Colonel," said Meade. "I just didn't understand —"

"Take the rest of day, Corporal," interrupted North with a caring smile. "That's an order."

"Yes, sir," replied Meade. "But I can take the hover train like normal."

"Nonsense," said North. "It's no trouble for Captain." He turned his gaze toward Burns. "Is it?"

"Not at all, Colonel," replied Burns who then placed his hand on Meade's shoulder. "Don't worry, Corporal, we'll take good care of you."

North saw a hint of hesitation in Meade.

"Thank you, Colonel," she said. "But it's really not —"

"Now Kelly," interrupted North, using Meade's first name. "You know you're one of my favorites."

Meade gave him a coy smile.

"And I want to take care of my favorites," added North.

"Yes, sir," replied Meade.

"Excellent. Then you just go with Mr. Burns and Mr. Miles and try to relax and forget about today."

"Yes, sir," said Meade, rising to her feet.

"That's my girl," said North. "Now you go with Lieutenant Miles while Captain Burns and I discuss some other matters."

Meade smiled and walked toward Miles, who escorted her out of the room.

As the door slid shut, Burns turned toward North. "Well, that's a damn shame."

"Just make it quick," said North. "And she's got family so make it look like a mugging or break in…we don't want the attention of a missing person."

"You're the boss," replied Burns. "How bad to you want it to look? Do you want us to —"

"No!" North let out a grunt of frustration. "Just make it look like some idiot got in over their head." He paused again. "And Burns … I was serious when I said make it quick."

Burns smiled. "You know me boss…always the professional."

"Make sure you are," warned North. "Neither one of us want Dzu to get concerned about how we handle things here."

Burns expression tightened. "I make sure it's done right."

North nodded and Burns exited to join Meade and Miles.

As the door closed again, North activated his tablet and began scanning through photos of potential medical technicians.

Chapter 4

Cathis, still in uniform, stood dead still in the park by the Seattle-Tacoma metro-city hover train station. The shriek of seagulls echoed over the water as she watched two children play in a pool with their mother looking on, her gaze locked on the two children as they splashed and laughed.

The image of two girls looking up at her in a bunker far away from Earth flashed through her mind.

Shaking her head, she shifted her attention to the mother. If they only knew what happened off-Earth to keep them safe.

Another flashback.

This time it was the image of the woman and child running across a field of yellow flowers that exploded into Cathis' conscious.

But then it was gone.

Cathis' stomach tightened. Her heart rate increased — by five beats per minute, her blood pressure spiked, and her temperature began to slowly rise point one degree Fahrenheit per hour. She closed her eyes trying to recall the image that had caused her physiological response.

"Hey!"

Cathis opened her eyes as Kayla approached. Kayla, in a shimmering yellow summer dress, almost floated toward her. Thin, brunette, and with an angelic face, she represented everything that Cathis no longer was — and everything she was fighting to protect.

"Hi, Michelle…I mean, Cathis," she said with a smile.

"You're late," responded Cathis. She was late after all.

Kayla sighed. "Am I too late to give my big sister a hug?" she asked, stepping toward Cathis with her arms extended.

Cathis opened her arms.

Kayla hugged her tight…as tight as a small, non-enhanced woman could.

Cathis slowly put her arms around Kayla's torso, barely making contact.

After a few seconds, two point two exactly, which felt like an eternity for Cathis, she opened her arms again. Kayla, recognizing the signal, broke her embrace.

"I didn't mean to be short," said Cathis. "Sometime the interface —"

"Don't worry about it," replied Kayla. "I'm just glad you're okay." Kayla's jaw tightened. "I have been so worried. They told me you'd been injured but wouldn't say anything else."

"I'm fine now," replied Cathis.

"What happened?"

"I got shot in the head. But it worked out for the best."

"What?" gasped Kayla. "How does getting shot work out for the best?"

"I can't say."

"How did it happen?"

"You know I can't tell you that either," said Cathis.

Kayla exhaled heavily. "Well, I just wish you didn't have to go out there."

"Someone has to."

"But why?"

"So that what happens there doesn't have to happen here."

"I…I guess…" Kayla paused, looking over Cathis. "Why are you still in your uniform? Aren't we going to dinner?"

"Yes. And what else would I wear?" asked Cathis. She had worn nothing but uniforms for the last five years.

The small communications device on Kayla's wrist beeped and a hologram of a man in a waiter's uniform appeared next to her.

"Your table will be ready in five minutes, Miss Harper," said the waiter.

"Perfect," replied Kayla with a smile. "We're on our way."

The hologram ended.

"He was cute," said Kayla.

"What?"

"He was…never mind." Kayla took Cathis' hand. "Let's go eat."

Cathis allowed Kayla to take her hand and drag her up the walkway to the nearby restaurant.

"It's just right over there," said Kayla as she reached the top of the platform. "Third one on the right, with the big yellow sign."

Cathis viewed the street as they walked toward the restaurant. The power used to light that single block of signs and holograms could power a deep space outpost for a week.

They reached the exterior and a handsome young waiter walked up to them.

"Miss Harper," said the waiter. "I'm Jonathan and I'll be your waiter."

"It's nice to meet you, Jonathan," replied Kayla.

Cathis scanned the exterior of the restaurant as Kayla and the waiter began to engage in small talk.

White walls and furniture accented with chrome set the theme as yellow-hued holograms of meal options slowly rotated in three columns by the entrance. The scene was so antiseptic it reminded Cathis of the CAT medical facility.

She glanced at a large screen making up one of the walls on the building next to the restaurant. It was playing a Consolidated Armaments Technologies commercial. Battle cruisers drifted in space before flashing to a formation of OE SOS infantry snapping to attention. *'Cannon fodder,'* she thought to herself. The screen then shifted to a family having a picnic on the grass as three atmo fighters flashed over-head. The boy looked up and turned to his dad. "I wanna be like them," declared the boy. "Someday," said the father with a smile, patting the boy on the head. "Someday." The image changed to a shot of OE SOS infantry, fleet, air, and logistics soldiers standing in front of the family. CAT — GOING UP THERE TO KEEP YOU SAFE DOWN HERE rolled across the screen.

Cathis smiled. No one would ever see a picture of her team.

"I have a seat for you two ladies right over here," said the waiter, his focus still completely on Kayla. "Miss Harper, I must say that you look love —"

"No," replied Cathis.

"No?" asked Kayla.

"That table won't do," said Cathis.

"But it's such a nice evening, don't you want to sit outside?"

"We'll sit there," said Cathis pointing to a table near the far corner.

Kayla sighed. "But wouldn't it be nicer —"

The waiter, coming to Kayla's aid, interrupted. "Miss Harper's reservation specifically called for —"

"Good views of the entrance and the door to the kitchen with a nearby exit. We sit there," said Cathis, ending the conversation as she started moving toward her table of choice.

As she moved, the light reflected off of her C.A.T.H.I.S. program insignia.

"Oh…uh, yes…ma'am. I…" stammered the waiter, finally realizing she was a C.A.T.H.I.S. "You're a Consolidated Armaments Technologies …"

"Human Interface Soldier," added Kayla. "But don't worry —"

"What I am is hungry," interrupted Cathis. "Let's go."

"Yes, uh …"

"Captain," said Cathis.

"Yes, Captain. I'm sorry. It's just…I've never met a —"

"If you don't get us to that table now, you'll never get the chance to meet another one of us," she added, her gaze locked onto the waiter as she motioned for him to move. Cathis noted Kayla rolling her eyes, but it didn't matter. She was hungry and the waiter had been too busy flirting with Kayla to get them seated.

Cathis and Kayla followed the waiter as he hustled to the table. Once there, the waiter pulled out Kayla's chair and helped her sit. He turned toward Cathis, but she was already seated.

"Uhm, yes. If you ladies would like some time to —"

"I'm ready," said Cathis.

"Don't you want to look at the menu?" asked Kayla.

"No need," replied Cathis, turning her gaze toward the waiter. "What meal has the most protein?"

"That would be our beef steak plate —"

"How many grams?"

"The steak?" asked the waiter.

"Of protein," said Cathis.

"Uh, I believe seventeen."

"And your largest carbohydrate plate?"

"We have a pasta dish with —"

"Grams?"

The waiter quickly scanned his tablet. "Thirty-seven."

"Is the beef real or synthesized?"

"You can choose."

"I'll take two beef plates, real, and a plate of the pasta."

"For yourself?" asked the waiter.

"Yes," replied Cathis. "That's what I asked for."

"Of course," said the waiter, turning toward Kayla. "And you, Miss Harper?"

"I guess I'll have the garden salad and a glass of white wine," she replied.

"Very good," said the waiter, turning back toward Cathis. "And what would you like to drink, Captain?"

"Do you have any whiskey?"

"No. I'm sorry but —"

"Then I'll take thirty-two ounces of water."

"Uh, ma'am," fumbled the waiter, "we have sixteen-ounce glasses and —"

"Well, then bring me two glasses."

"Of course."

The waiter stood silent, unsure if they were done.

"You can go," said Cathis.

"Of course," he replied, scurrying off.

Cathis turned her attention back to the table. "Jesus, that was difficult."

"Why did you order so much food?" asked Kayla.

"My metabolism is higher than yours Kayla. And I'm only at…" She paused, accessing her interface. "…eighty-nine percent of tactical strength. So I need more fuel to keep healing."

"I guess," said Kayla. "But why did you have to…" Kayla stopped mid-sentence.

"What? What did I have to what?"

"Never mind," replied Kayla. "It's not important. Let's just enjoy our meal."

***

As Cathis finished her second steak, Kayla put her fork on the table and leaned in toward her sister. "Can I ask you something?"

"Of course," replied Cathis, still chewing the last bite of the steak.

"What was that about … with the waiter?"

Cathis guffawed. "Oh, c'mon. Is that what's had you bothered this whole time? I was just having a little fun. And I was starving. Do you know how long it's been since I've had real food?"

"Have you looked around the room?"

Cathis blinked to confirm what she already knew. "Ten men, twelve women, and three children. Those are the customers. The staff consists of the manager, two cooks, two waitresses, and your little waiter friend. None of them pose a threat to our meal if —"

"They're terrified of you," snapped Kayla, rapidly lowering her voice, trailing into a whisper.

Cathis glanced around the room. Most were either staring at her and Kayla or intentionally avoiding eye contact.

"You could kill everyone in this room, and they know it…or at least that's what the recruitment ads and commercials say."

"But I won't. It's my job to protect them," replied Cathis. Now it was her lowering her voice. "Don't they know that?"

Kayla glanced up toward the ceiling as she prepared for a conversation that had become too familiar. "Why did the waiter have to seat us based on the tactical situation of this restaurant? We're on Earth. Not Titan, or Mars, or some asteroid. And you purposely scared the waiter."

"If it only took a few words and a harsh look to scare him, that's not my problem," huffed Cathis. "If I'd really wanted to scare him —"

"See," interrupted Kayla. "That's what I mean. Not every interaction has to be contest for dominance."

"That's exactly what they are, Kayla."

"Maybe for you but not for normal…" She stopped. "I mean —"

"I can't just turn this off," replied Cathis, her gut tightening. She didn't like these conversations either; it's exactly why she hadn't planned on seeing Kayla in the first place. "You have no idea what happens out there. And if you think that anywhere is *really* safe, you need to —"

"Don't we ever get to be normal?" Kayla leaned in closer, gritting her teeth before continuing. "Normal people don't act like this. Normal people don't talk like this." She exhaled. "Normal people don't change their names… don't you remember the way you were before you —"

"Yes," interrupted Cathis. Kayla had asked, so she'd tell her. "I was weak. I was afraid and unprepared. I was —"

"You were Michelle!" Kayla paused, taking a deep breath. "I'm sorry. I didn't mean to…"

"I know you want me to be the big sister I was before. But I can't be … not anymore." Damn her for starting this. "They took that away."

"The military?"

"Of course not. That night… when they…"

The soft warmth of Kayla's hands covered Cathis' right hand. "We don't need to talk about that now. We don't ever need to talk about it … unless you want to?"

Cathis closed her eyes. Her heart rate spiked and her temperature rose as the night that changed everything flashed through her memory. "There's nothing to talk about, Kayla. They did what they did…," She swallowed hard. "…and I did what I had to do in order to make sure it never happens again."

"Cathis…I…"

"I'm sorry, Kayla. I know you feel like you've lost a part of your sister." Cathis straightened her body and placed her palms on the table. "But the truth is, what was left of Michelle wasn't worth keeping."

A tear rolled down Kayla's cheek as she looked down at the table.

Cathis, despite how much she didn't want to acknowledge emotions, could feel Kayla's heart breaking.

"Do you really believe that?" asked Kayla as she focused her tear-filled eyes onto Cathis.

Cathis had no answer other than the one she had given.

"But I don't need a soldier," pleaded Kayla. "I need a sister."

Cathis leaned in toward her sister. "Everyone needs a soldier. They just don't know it."

***

Kayla and Cathis walked in silence down the dimly lit street after dinner.

Cathis fumed. This is how their last two visits had ended and she just didn't see the point anymore. But she also couldn't refuse her sister. After all, it had been Kayla that had stayed with her and helped when it happened. Cathis, then Michelle, had never been more vulnerable than those long painful days and Kayla was the only thing that got her through it. Maybe it was her debt to let her sister remind her of who she used to be…even if Cathis never wanted to be that person again.

"This is ridiculous," said Kayla, breaking Cathis' reflection on their relationship.

"What?"

"I don't mean to frustrate you and I know — at least I think — you don't mean to frustrate me. Let's not talk about any of that stuff for the rest of the night." Kayla smiled.

"That's probably a good idea," said Cathis.

Kayla looked past Cathis. "Let's just go have some fun."

"Fun?"

"Yeah, fun." Kayla titled her head. "You do remember how to have fun, right?"

Actually, she didn't. "What do you want to do?"

"Over there," replied Kayla, pointing toward an entrance to a club. "Just some dancing and some drinks?"

Was she serious? "I don't dance. Not anymore."

Kayla tugged on Cathis' arm. "C'mon. We'll just go in for a minute. What do you do when you're out there for fun?"

"It's not 'fun' out there, Kayla," replied Cathis.

"This could be good for you…to actually relax," said Kayla, tugging on Cathis' arm. "I'm sure they'll have whiskey in there."

Cathis examined the situation. The thump of techno music echoed from the building with a sign that read: GOOD TIMES. A large bouncer in a shirt that was too tight…and pants that were really too tight, watched the door as people shuffled in and out. He was well-muscled but Cathis could tell he was not flexible and probably not very coordinated…just a hunk of meat to scare the patrons into behaving.

"I really don't understand why you want to go in there."

"Wouldn't it be nice to just not think about…anything for a while? Let's just get a drink and see if the music changes your mind?" asked Kayla, giving another gentle tug.

'*I guess a drink wouldn't be bad*,' though Cathis. "Sure."

"Great!" said Kayla with a bounce. "But let's take this off," she added, reaching for the C.A.T.H.I.S. insignia on Cathis' uniform.

Cathis brought her hand up to stop her. "What are you doing?"

"No need to freak everyone out," she said, confidently sliding the insignia off of her uniform. "See…no big bad wolf."

"Whatever," said Cathis, already regretting her decision. "Can we get this over with?"

Cathis followed Kayla as she bounded toward the massive bouncer at the door.

Kayla stopped at the entrance, looking up toward the bouncer towering over her.

"Verification," said the man in a deep, guttural voice.

Cathis fought back a chuckle.

"Here," said Cathis, extending her arm to present her wrist communications device.

"Confirm owner and age," said the bouncer into the device.

An obedient response followed. "Ownership confirmed. Kayla Harper. Age twenty-four."

The bouncer turned toward Cathis. "You're good if you're in uniform."

"Thanks," chirped Kayla, pulling Cathis inside.

The thumping instantly shifted to a percussive rhythm that rippled across Cathis' body. *'Not unlike close air support,'* she thought.

Her vision instantly adjusted to the light as she searched the crowded club for potential threats.

"C'mon, let's dance," said Kayla. "You used to love to dance."

Cathis stood, immovable.

"I…I can't," said Cathis. "I'm sorry."

"Maybe we should go," said Kayla. "I just wanted us to —"

"Dancing always made you happy," interrupted Cathis, saying the words to herself more than Kayla. "We can stay…" offered Cathis, "… for a little bit."

"Really?"

Cathis nodded. "Sure. You dance…I'll be at the bar. After you've danced a bit, we can maybe talk…"

"Okay," said Kayla with a wide smile. "Get me a drink. I'm gonna dance a bit … then we'll talk."

"Fine," replied Cathis, turning toward the bar. But she stopped, gripping Kayla's arm. "I'll be watching if you need me."

"Okay," chuckled Kayla, before gamboling her way to the dance floor.

As Kayla danced, Cathis made her way to the bar. A fit, dark haired man in yet another tight shirt greeted her from behind the bar.

"Hello, cutie," he said with a smile, yelling over the music. "What can I get you?"

"A whiskey and some kind of fruity drink," she replied.

"How about I get that for you?" came a voice from behind her.

Cathis turned to see a tall, blonde man with deep blue eyes staring at her. *'When did Earth stop making normal sized shirts?'* she thought looking at the man. "Excuse me?"

"I just thought a pretty lady — I mean soldier — like yourself shouldn't have to pay for her own drinks."

"Sure," replied Cathis.

"Great," said the man, extending his wrist communicator to pay for the drinks.

Taking the drinks, he handed them to Cathis.

"Who's the whiskey for? Hopefully not a boyfriend?"

"No. It's mine."

"Oh, badass," he said. "And the other drink?"

"My sister," replied Cathis, pointing to Kayla, who had already attracted two men.

Cathis focused on the men as they moved around her. Both were tall, over six foot and at least two hundred pounds. One was blonde with hair down to his shoulders and the other had his hair cut close to his scalp. They dwarfed Kayla as they circled her like two wolves around a lamb. Kayla noticed the men and motioned for them to dance with her.

"Jesus," huffed Cathis.

"She's pretty hot too," said the man standing next to Cathis. "Must run in the family."

The man brushed his hand over Cathis' forearm, which she quickly pulled away.

"My name's Ronald —"

"Thanks for the drinks, Ronald," interrupted Cathis.

"But don't you want to —"

"No, Ronald. I don't," replied Cathis, her eyes staring defiantly at him. "You can go now."

"C'mon, now," he huffed, as he ran his hand over her the back of her upper arm. He leaned in close. "I like the attitude…goes with the uniform," he said, the warmth of his breath washing over her skin. "I bet I could touch you in places that would make you scream."

Cathis fought off the repulsion and forced a smile. "Really?"

Ronald returned her smile. "I know it … if you just —"

Cathis turned, and with one hand, grabbed him and shoved him against the bar in a controlled manner that didn't bring attention to them. As he struggled to get free, she stepped in close to him.

"I know some special places on the body too," she said, her eyes locked on his. "Right here, under the jaw," she continued, pressing her finger against his neck under his jaw causing him to wince. "Carotid artery and jugular vein are right there. Just slide a blade in about one-point-five inches and you'll start to fade in about ten seconds."

"Hey, I didn't —"

"Shhh, baby," she whispered, placing her index finger to his lips. "You wanted to talk…and I'm not done."

Next, she slid her hand to his throat. "Here, you still get the jugular although it will be a bit slower. But if you do it right, the trachea, larynx, and ligaments holding your head all get severed too so you're bleeding out, suffocating, and can't scream."

"Please," he begged.

Cathis gripped his neck, squeezing tight. She saw his face turn purple and lessened her grip slightly. "Still not done, Ronald," she said through her teeth.

Her hand slid down his torso. "The heart and lungs are obvious but here…" She ran her hand over his abdomen and looked down at his torso. "Now everyone knows a nice long, deep cut here will spill your guts on the deck but…" She returned her gaze to his wide eyes. "What they don't realize is that when that abdominal wall gets sliced the right way, you pretty much can't move your body in any normal way…you just kinda flop around, waving your arms and legs with your intestines spilling out on the floor." She raised to her tiptoes and whispered in his ear. "And I don't even need a knife to do it."

She took a step back, still holding him in place. "Now those aren't the only special places I know about, but they are some of my favorites." She released him. "Want to hear about the others?"

Ronald turned without a word and scurried away. "Crazy bitch," he mumbled when he thought he was out of ear shot.

Cathis placed her drink on the table to follow him but stopped when her attention was drawn to Kayla on the dance floor.

The two men had moved in close, one in front and one behind her. They began to press against her, one of them running his hand down her side to her hips.

Kayla brushed his hand away but continued dancing, smiling.

The other man pressed his hips against Kayla's and wrapped his hands around her waist.

Cathis felt her combat interface begin to initiate as Kayla's expression changed and she pushed the man's hands away.

The first man put his hand to her cheek, but Kayla blocked his touch. Her senses focused,

Cathis heard Kayla say, "I said, no!" over the loud music before quickly exiting the dance floor.

Cathis was locked onto the men when she met Kayla halfway across the floor.

"Are you okay?" she asked, glancing down at Kayla.

"I'm fine, Cathis," said Kayla, clearly realizing Cathis' intent. "They're just jerks. It happens all the time."

"Not tonight." Cathis turned toward the men, who were now looking in their direction.

Cathis felt Kayla's arm grasp her uniform.

"No, Cathis. Really, I'm fine. You're right; this was a bad idea. Let's just go."

Cathis didn't reply. She was locked onto her prey.

"Cathis!" shouted Kayla, finally drawing her attention. "Please."

"Fine," grumbled Cathis. "Let's go," she said, casting one more challenging glance toward the two men.

***

As they stepped out of the club, a light rain had started fall. The few people on the street had activated their personal shields with their wrist devices to shelter them from the drizzle.

Cathis didn't notice the rain; her body was on fire. The jerk at the bar had been fun to fuck with, but it also activated her tactical interface, sending adrenaline coursing through her body. That, combined with the two assholes putting their hands on Kayla, had her wound tight.

"Great," huffed Kayla, hunching her shoulders as the rain hit the back of her neck. "You can share mine," she continued, knowing Cathis didn't wear a device.

"I'm fine. It's just a little rain," she said as they stepped into the street. Maybe the rain would cool her off.

"Hey, bitch!" came a voice from behind them.

Cathis turned to see that the two men from the dance floor had followed them outside.

A smile came to her face.

"Just go back inside and leave us alone," said Kayla.

"You can't tease us like that," said the blonde-haired man.

"I wasn't…" Kayla glanced nervously toward Cathis. "Just go. You really *need* to leave us alone."

"I don't think so," said the short-haired man. "You think it's funny, spinnin' us up like that then walking away?"

"You need to shut the fuck up, asshole," said Cathis, standing in front of Kayla.

"Whoa," chuckled the long-haired man. "That one's a tease and this one's a cunt."

"Yeah," added the short-haired man, but they're both hot," he said, looking toward Cathis. "I bet the soldier girl is…firm."

The short-haired man stepped toward Cathis.

"Cathis, no," pleaded Kayla from behind her.

The short-haired man raised his hand, pointing toward Kayla. "You just need to be taught —"

Cathis landed a boot to the man's chest that sent him flying backwards.

"What the fuck?" shouted the long-haired man as he reached into his pocket and pulled out a knife.

"No!" screamed Kayla as the long-haired man lunged at Cathis.

Cathis grabbed the man's wrist and wretched it backwards with a snap before landing a blow to his jaw, knocking him unconscious.

"Stop!" shouted the bouncer as he rushed forward, placing his hand on Cathis' shoulder.

Cathis spun around and landed a blow to his ribs.

The sound of ribs cracking was drowned out by the bouncer's scream.

"Cathis!" shouted Kayla as she shrank away from the destruction.

Still holding the bouncer's arm, she drove her boot into his knee, snapping it and sending him to the ground. She pivoted, cupped the back of his head and, with a grunt, sent him flying against a wall ten feet away.

She didn't notice the drizzle had turned to a downpour as she turned toward the short-haired man who was slowly rising to his feet.

"Get away!" warned the man, raising his fists to defend himself as Cathis strode toward him.

The man swung with his right arm but Cathis grabbed it and extended it outward as she shifted her body to the left. "Who's the cunt now?" she asked with a smile, bringing her knee upward while driving his arm down.

The short-haired man's arm snapped like a piece of kindling and he fell to the ground in agony.

Cathis looked up toward Kayla. She had backed herself against a nearby wall in horror. Her hands were over her mouth, unable to move.

Cathis sensed movement then turned toward the long-haired man, who was regaining consciousness.

She picked up his knife and knelt over him.

"No. Please," he begged.

"Not quite the result you expected?" she asked, pulling his face to within inches of hers. "Thought you were a badass, eh?" She slammed him back onto the ground, pinning him with one hand. "We'll you fucked with the top of food chain tonight, you little prick."

"Cathis! Please!" shouted Kayla once she had recovered enough to run to her sister. "You don't have to hurt them anymore," she pleaded, tugging at Cathis' shoulder.

Cathis glanced up toward Kayla, her eyes on fire. "I'm not gonna hurt him." She turned back toward the man. "I'm just gonna skin him alive," she said with a smile as she placed the knife to his cheek.

"Please," begged the man.

"Cathis. No," added Kayla.

Cathis looked deep into the man's eyes. He was a coward. And even if he wasn't, he was no match for her. She could've killed all three of them in half the time she'd spent playing with her prey. "Fine," she said, tossing the knife into the darkness and standing.

She snatched the man off the ground, holding him in the air with one hand. "Bitch," she said before landing another blow, knocking him unconscious again.

Cathis turned back toward Kayla. "I'm done."

The chirp of a siren and a blinding light drew her attention from the man at her feet.

Two police officers stepped out of a patrol hover, the spotlight from their car focused on the carnage in front of them.

"Get your hands up!" ordered the first officer.

Cathis' vision powered through the light and the rain. The officer was holding a Mark-3 sidearm. The ten standard eight millimeter round wouldn't slow her down unless he got a few good headshots. No doubt the other was armed with the same. She had already planned her attack when she looked toward Kayla. Her arms were already in the air and her body shook from the cold rain and fear.

"You too!" shouted the second officer toward Cathis. "Raise your fucking arms!"

Cathis glanced toward the officer, then back to Kayla. She didn't think her sister could take seeing any more violence.

Cathis slowly raised her arms.

The first officer holstered his pistol and moved toward them.

"What the hell happened here?" he asked.

"They bit off a little more than they could chew," replied Cathis, a smile painted on her drenched face.

"Let's see you're IDs," said the second officer.

Kayla extended her wrist device, which the officer scanned. A soft *beep* verified her information.

"You too," he said, looking toward Cathis.

Cathis lowered her arms and rolled up her left sleeve to display a bar code. "Here ya go."

The officer glanced up toward Cathis, his brow furrowed, before running the scanner over the tattoo.

"They're still alive," said the first officer. "But they're pretty messed up. I'll call it in."

"You know you're gonna get in a lot of trouble on the base for this," warned the second officer.

The scanner let out a shrill tone and the officer looked down to read the data.

"I doubt it," said Cathis.

The officer looked back up toward Cathis, his jaw slacked. "I…" He turned toward his partner then back to Cathis. "You are free to go."

"What the hell are you talking about?" asked the partner. "Look at this mess."

"We don't have jurisdiction," replied the officer, showing the scanner display to his partner.

"What the hell?" mumbled the first officer looking at the readout. "No data…classified by Head of Department OE SOS.

"She's a C.A.T.H.I.S.," declared the second officer.

Cathis saw the first officer's hand slide back toward his pistol. "Are we free to go or not?" she asked.

"Yes. Go. Please," replied the first officer.

"I don't understand," said Kayla. "Why —"

"They don't want to bite off more than they can chew, either."

Kayla looked back at the three broken bodies. "What about them?"

"We'll take care it," said the second officer. "Just go."

***

Again they walked in silence, this time drenched, until they reached Kayla's apartment. At the door, Kayla turned to Cathis. "You should come in. We need to talk about what happened."

"You don't really want to, Kayla."

"I do," she said defiantly. "Those men. What you did to them."

"That?" Cathis scoffed. "They got off lucky."

"Lucky? You almost killed them —" She paused. "You *were* going to kill them. Why?"

Cathis' stomach tightened and her skin grew hot. "What do you mean, why?" Did Kayla really not understand? After everything they…that Michelle…had been through. "People like that get to walk around and do whatever they like…and they get away with it because no one stops them."

"Cathis, I —"

"And no one stops them because they're sheep; you're all sheep. And that's why you, why every one of you, need people like me."

Kayla took a step backwards before exhaling heavily. A faint, hopeful smile comes to her face.

"But you didn't kill them."

"Because of you," huffed Cathis. "I could have snapped their necks and been done with it. Maybe that's what I should have done." She paused wondering why she hadn't just killed them. "I guess I wanted to play with my food a little."

"What?" gasped Kayla.

"You know, blow off some steam."

Kayla steadied herself for what she was about to say. "I can't keep doing this."

"Doing what?" asked Cathis.

"I can't keep pretending that you're my…that you're the person you were before."

"Kayla, we've been through this —"

"No, Cathis!" interrupted Kayla. "You listen to me now. When they shoved all that shit into your body, they made you —"

"They made me better!"

"No!" whimpered Kayla, no longer able to hold back her tears. "They made you less human."

Cathis stared at Kayla blankly. She felt the warmth of a tear running down her cheek and quickly wiped it away. "I'm gonna have to talk to the doc about that."

"About what?" asked Kayla.

"This tear thing. It keeps happening and I have no idea why."

Kayla stepped inside of her apartment and looked up toward the ceiling. Letting out a sigh, she returned her gaze to Cathis. "That's all that's left of my sister. And you're gonna give them that too," she said before closing the door.

Cathis stood silent, staring at the door. Why didn't Kayla understand that she'd only done what needed to be done? If she hadn't been there, those men could have…she should have killed them. "Damn it," she cursed, raising her hand to knock on Kayla's door so she could tell her just what men like that were capable of doing.

She paused as a series of images exploded through her head.

A field of yellow flowers and a woman and a child.

An old man speaking Arabic.

A column of armored hover cars burning on a mountain road.

And a dozen other images that made no sense to her.

The parade of images stopped with the vision of two girls staring up at her.

"Fuck." Cathis leaned against the wall of the hallway, trying to piece together the random flashes. She needed to rest, maybe not physically but definitely mentally.

By the time she'd reached the outside of Kayla's building, her body was tense with anxiety over the way they had parted…and the unexplained flood of images that had run through her mind.

With no other release available, she started to run.

She focused on her breathing, the pounding of her feet, and the rhythmic motion of her arms and legs as she was soon at a full sprint.

Twenty-seven miles per hour.

The vision of those men putting their hands on Kayla on the dance floor ran through her mind.

She pushed harder.

Twenty-eight miles per hour.

Her mind flashed back even further, as she struggled against strong hands holding her down on her bed.

"Fuck," she grunted, pushing even harder each time her feet hit the ground.

Twenty-nine miles per hour.

She flew past people standing on the street as she ran … she didn't know if it was toward something or away from something…but she ran.

In the distance she saw a mother and a young girl standing outside of a small shop. Instead of slowing, she pushed even harder.

Thirty miles per hour.

Her vision focused on the two, now two hundred yards ahead and closing fast.

Suddenly the street was covered with waist-high yellow flowers.

She felt rage course through her body as she reached for blade in a tactical vest that she was not wearing.

"No!" The word exploded in her consciousness and she slid to a stop.

Five feet in front of her was a woman, holding a bag of groceries in one hand and clutching her young daughter's hand with the other. Both had wide eyes as they had looked up to see Cathis barreling toward them only for her to suddenly stop.

"I…I'm sorry," said Cathis, feeling an unexplainable weight of guilt. "I didn't mean to scare you."

The woman pulled her daughter closer. "You should be more careful out here running in the dark," said the mother. "Shouldn't you be exercising on the base or something?"

"Oh…yes." The base — that's where she needed to go…where she belonged.

***

Cathis tried not to think about Kayla or anything that had happened that night as she sat on the ferry heading back the CAT medical facility. Sitting alone, she ran through technical specifications of each infantry weapon and … she looked down at the deck to see a series of patterns printed on them. Shifting her focus, she began to calculate the angles.

"Didn't think I'd see you out here," came a voice from behind her.

Cathis spun around to see Greeves standing over her.

"What are you doing?" she asked.

"Probably the same thing you are…headed back to the facility."

"Yep," replied Cathis. "Where I belong."

"Rough day with your sister?" asked Greeves.

"How did you know I —"

"I do know you have a sister that lives here," said Greeves. "She is literally the only thing about Earth you have ever mentioned, if only once or twice."

Cathis let out a sigh. "It went as expected."

He placed his hand on her shoulder. "None of them, including your sister, are ever going to understand us," he said as he sat next to her. "But that's the price we pay."

Cathis nodded in acknowledgement. "Well, sometimes it sucks."

"Well, you know the answer to that, Captain."

"Embrace the suck," they said in unison.

"Exactly," continued Greeves. "They are able to bounce around from one party to the next, to bitch about their office jobs, to fucking hydro-surf…all because of what we do out there."

Cathis chuckled. "You sound like a fucking recruiting video, First Sergeant."

"That's because I am walking recruitment ad, Captain," he said, opening his arms as if to present himself. "And so are you."

"I know what we do is important. You don't have to sell me," she replied. She exhaled heavily. "I just fucking hate being on Earth," declared Cathis. "They're so oblivious…so entitled…so weak."

"They can be weak because you're strong." He leaned in close. "I mean it. What you've become…who you are now. You *are* the apex predator in this entire Solar System." He stood as the ferry slid into its mooring. "It's not your fault, nor should it be your concern, if the common man doesn't fucking understand you."

Cathis rose to her feet.

He was right. All of the bullshit that had happened earlier in the day…it was just bad from an Earther's perspective. A perspective that had no comprehension of what warfare – what true savagery – actually looked like.

"Fuck it," said Cathis. "I'll be cleared tomorrow and then I'll be on my way back out there…where all of this will just be a bad memory."

Chapter 5

Cathis sat upright on the examination table at the CAT facility. Next to her were Colonel North, the medical technician Michael, and a new, but attractive female medical tech. The guard that took up a post just outside the door did not skip her attention either.

"All right, Captain," said Colonel North. "Last test before you're cleared for duty."

"Then let's get it over with, Colonel. I've had all the R&R I can take."

"We heard about your little scuffle last night," said North. "If that's what you mean by R&R?"

Cathis laughed. "My idea of R&R would have been to pull their hearts out through their chests with them watching."

"Well, it's a good thing you didn't or we'd have to deal with a whole lot more paperwork," said North.

"Paperwork's not my problem," said Cathis.

"I guess it's not," said North, turning toward his new medical tech. "Has the diagnostic completed?"

"Yes, Colonel," replied the technician with a flirtatious smile.

North gave a nod to Michael, who inserted a small chip into the port in the back of Cathis' head.

As he did, he leaned in close. "It will all be clear soon. Trust me," he whispered.

Confused, Cathis looked up toward him but Michael had already turned his attention to Colonel North.

"Ready, Colonel," reported Michael.

***

North looked down at the tablet in his hand. On it was a rendering of Cathis' body, highlighting vital organs and the various enhancements she had undergone over the years. He tapped on the drop-down menu and selected VALIDATE DOWNLOAD WIPE, then EXECUTE.

The screen flashed red, displaying the word FAULT as a shrill tone echoed through the room.

***

Cathis' muscles spasmed as she convulsed.

Suddenly, her mind exploded with memories: Her and Kayla playing as children. Her comforting a seventeen-year-old Kayla at their mother's funeral.

***

"What's happening?" asked the shocked medical tech. "This isn't normal, is it?"

"I don't know," said Michael glancing toward North, who kept pressing tabs on the tablet.

"Damn it. She won't shut down," cursed North.

***

Cathis' memories continued to flood her.

She saw herself in graduate school, still Michelle, talking to an attractive young man. Then that young man, along with two others standing in front of the door of her dorm room, blocking her exit.

She saw, no felt, herself try to run past them but the man picked her up, throwing her onto the bed, forcing the air from her lungs.

"No," she begged, looking up at them as they stood over her.

***

"Get in here!" shouted Colonel North for the guard.

The guard stepped inside, bringing his rifle to the ready.

"Stand by, damn it!" ordered North.

***

Cathis' memory shifted to her lying in a medical bed, beaten and bruised, as Kayla held her hand.

Then to her sitting on her couch covering herself in a blanket, alone and shaking in fear as a delivery man continuously knocked on the door.

She saw herself reading her release from her doctorate program for failure to attend class.

Then…her looking up toward North on the 115th floor of federal building.

'Do you want to be a lamb for the rest of your life…or do you want to be a lion?' echoed North's voice.

***

"Son of a bitch," grunted North as he tried in vain to shut down Cathis as she continued to convulse.

***

Now Cathis' memories took her to basic training and the laboratory procedures she willingly endured as part of the C.A.T.H.I.S. program.

Another flash and she was running, then shooting, then fighting hand-to-hand as her training continued.

Her memory jumped to that beautiful field of flowers. Cathis felt the blood and mud on her face as she closed in on the woman and child running from her. In her memory she could see bodies spread across the field. The woman stumbles and falls. Cathis raises her knife...

***

"Why isn't she responding?" asked the medical tech, backing away from the examination table.

The guard moved closer to Cathis as her unconscious body shook involuntarily.

***

Cathis was now standing in the middle of the field. She held her hands to her face; they were coated in blood, her right hand still gripping the blood-soaked knife.

In the distance, a yellow farm house was engulfed in flames. She looked up toward a flagpole by the house. An American flag flapped in the wind as smoke billowed from the structure.

Looking down at her feet, she saw the mangled bodies of the woman and the child …

***

Cathis' eyes opened and she shot up from the examination table. Her gaze fixed on the guard, wide-eyed as he raised his rifle to his shoulder.

Cathis kicked the rifle from the guard's hands just as he fired and landed a blow to his jaw, knocking him to the ground.

She sensed the female medical tech bolt for the door, but she was on her instantly. Cathis grabbed the woman's hair and slammed her backwards into the floor, knocking her unconscious.

She felt a pain register on her back, then her muscles spasm North activated the taser he had fired into her. Letting out a grunt and grimacing through the pain, she turned toward him.

North dropped the taser and slammed his tablet against the side of Cathis' head. Cathis absorbed the blow and faced him again.

"Stop!" he shouted.

Cathis torqued her body and crashed her foot into his left knee. North let out a scream and began to drop to the ground. As he fell, she grabbed the back of his uniform and tossed him across the room into the cabinets against the wall.

She spun back around just as the guard fired his pistol. The round tore into her right abdomen as she shifted her body. She looked down at the wound then back toward the guard.

The burst of automatic gunfire suddenly filled the room and the guard disappeared in a wave of bullets.

Cathis pivoted toward Michael, who'd fired the rifle.

"No!" he cried, dropping the rifle. "I'm no threat. I'm here to help you."

Cathis paused, staring at him. She panted as her mind raced with repressed memories and confusion and rage engulfed her. "What did you do to me?" she demanded.

"I showed you the truth," replied Michael, holding his hands in the air. "I gave you back the memories they were trying to keep from you."

"What are…I…" She paused again, shaking her head as more memories flooded her. Flashes of violence, of death, exploded in her mind. Unable to control them, she fell to her knees. "No. I didn't do that…I…I" She began to hyperventilate as tears poured down her cheeks.

"I can help you," offered Michael, moving toward her.

She jumped back to her feet into a defensive stance. "Stay the fuck away from me."

"Just let me help you. We need to get out of here."

"What is happening to me?"

"I can tell you everything…but we don't have time now. You need to come with me."

"Where? I can't leave —"

"You just attacked an OE SOS officer and the guard is dead," said Michael.

Cathis scanned the carnage she and Michael had caused.

"What do you think they will do to you?" continued Michael.

"Why did the guard try to shoot me? And Colonel North. He —"

"I promise you will understand but we *have* to go."

Cathis' mind raced. Nothing made sense. She closed her eyes and took in a deep breath. She knew one thing to be true…Michael was right, they'd kill her for this.

"Fuck," she cursed, looking back toward Michael. "Give me that rifle."

Michael picked up the rifle and handed it her.

Cathis checked the weapon's status and knelt next to the dead guard, pulling three magazines from his vest. "I'm assuming you have a plan … how do we get out of here?"

"Are you okay to move?" asked Michael, looking down at Cathis' gunshot wound.

She stared back at him.

"Okay. Follow me," he said, realizing the wound was a simple scratch to her.

Michael picked up the guard's pistol and moved toward the exit. He stepped into the hallway but froze when he felt a pistol pressed against his temple.

"Drop your weapon," came an order from a guard just outside the room.

Michael complied and turned back toward Cathis as the guard pushed him back into the room, positioning himself behind Michael for cover.

"You too!" demanded the guard to Cathis. "Drop your weapon or —"

The guard crumpled to the floor as Cathis sent a round through his forehead.

"Pick up your weapon," said Cathis to a dumbstruck Michael. "Damn it, this situation is so fucked."

She saw Michael, still shaken from having the pistol held to his head, gingerly pick up his pistol. "Maybe you should follow me … which way do we go?"

"You have the plans. I included them in the download that restored your memories, as well as a firewall that prevents CAT from shutting you down remotely or tracking you."

Cathis closed her eyes, allowing the interface to access the data.

"Where's our exit?" she asked, the facility blueprints now laid out in her head.

"We'll use the maintenance tunnels below the facility…then we move to grid 7-F."

Alarms began to blare.

"Shit," cursed Michael. "We have to —"

The piercing alarms triggered another flashback and Cathis doubled over as images of the savagery she had carried out again consumed her. She let out a guttural cough. "Why?"

"You're just remembering. Focus," said Michael. "You can work through it."

Cathis took a deep breath. The images faded. "Alright. Stay close and stay the fuck out of my way."

Cathis peered into the passageway only to be met with a hail of gunfire. Spinning back inside, she looked at Michael. "Be ready to move," she said as she stepped toward the dead guard. Grabbing the guard with one hand and lifting him off the ground, she returned to the door. "Follow me when I go."

She tossed the body into the passageway.

As gunfire erupted, Cathis dropped to her knees, pivoted, and sent a burst down the passageway, killing two guards to her right.

She spun toward the other direction just as Michael fired, killing another guard.

A nurse burst from behind a desk, running for safety.

Cathis raised her rifle but as she fired, Michael directed the barrel toward the ceiling.

"No!" he shouted.

"What the fuck?!" Cathis felt the rage and confusion bubbling over again.

"You don't have to kill everyone," said Michael. "She was —"

"C'mon," interrupted Cathis, as she turned and began moving down the passageway.

Moving quickly through the facility, they reached a door with a keypad lock.

Michael stepped in front of her. "It'll just take a second to —"

Cathis moved to her left and slammed her boot into the door, sending it flying open. "Open."

The two stepped into a dark room lined with multiple server arrays. In the center of the room was a heavy metallic hatch leading downward.

"You can't kick that one open," said Michael as he knelt by the hatch and began punching numbers into the keypad.

As he worked, another guard burst into the room but Cathis was ready.

She grabbed the man's arm and slammed him against the wall with a thud before knocking him unconscious. Cathis yanked the man off the floor and placed her arms around his neck, ready to break it.

Just before she applied pressure, she looked up toward Michael, who was returning her gaze.

"That's right. You don't have to kill him."

She let the guard fall back to the ground.

"Just open the damn hatch."

"Yes, Captain." A beep told Michael he was successful and he pulled the hatch open. "You first," he said, holding his arm toward the opening.

Cathis stepped to the edge and leapt in.

Hitting the ground, another flashback hit her. Cathis stumbled backwards, dropping her rifle. "No!" she yelled, holding her hands to her head. "No. No. No."

"Focus, Captain," said Michael, placing his hands over hers.

Cathis shoved him, sending him crashing into the wall.

He tried to regain his balance, but she was on him, pressing him against the concrete bricks.

"These…*things*…why didn't I remember doing them?" She stepped away. "Did I do them?" she asked, more tears streaming down her face.

"Just wait until we see Jacob. He can explain everything that is happening."

Cathis grabbed Michael's neck and lifted him off the floor. "Then what do I need you for? Stop fucking around and tell me what's happening."

Michael struggled but she was too strong. "L…let me…down…please."

Cathis released her grip and Michael fell to the ground. After regaining his breath, Michael stood. "We don't have time for this," he said, his voice scratchy and weak.

Cathis again shoved him against the wall, but this time allowed him to breath. "You tell me what's going on or only one of us is leaving this tunnel."

"All I know is Jacob told me to infiltrate the facility, upload the program, and bring you back to him if it worked."

Cathis didn't respond. She pressed against his chest a little more.

"He said your memories are important. That they can free us from the tyranny of the corporations."

She lessened the pressure. "What the fuck are you talking about?"

"That's all I know. I swear. If you want to know more, you have to talk to Jacob."

Cathis released Michael, stepping back. Her mind raced. She couldn't go back. Even if there were just some malfunction that had caused all of this, she'd killed OE SOS soldiers and possibly Colonel North…CAT would kill her as a defective unit or just to save face. But why did North attack her so quickly? "Shit," said Cathis. "Just to be clear, I don't fucking trust you…but I don't have any other options."

"Okay," said Michael. "We have to move. They'll find us if we stay here too long."

Cathis let out a heavy breath and picked up the rifle. "Fine. Take me to this Jacob."

***

Alarms continued to blare while medical teams carried away the dead guards and the unconscious medical tech. Colonel North, his knee shattered, hobbled to a screen next to the examination table.

"Colonel," asked a younger doctor. "Let me take a look —"

"No!" shouted North. "Get out."

"Sir?"

"Everyone get out!" he yelled.

As the room emptied, North turned back to the screen and activated it. There was a beep, then Mr. Dzu's face appeared.

"What happened?" asked Dzu.

"We don't know. As soon as we initiated the final scan, a fault code initiated."

Dzu leaned in to the screen. "Did she have recall?"

"No," lied North. "It was most likely a psychological break caused by an improper repair mixed with a faulty interface reboot."

"What the hell does that mean?"

"It means she's having a break from reality."

"Where is she?"

North didn't answer.

"Colonel? Where is she?"

"She escaped."

"What?" After a flurry of profanity in Chinese, Dzu again spoke English. "Why wasn't she shut down when this happened?"

"We attempted both local and remote shutdowns…she didn't respond."

Dzu leaned back in his chair and looked up toward the ceiling before returning his gaze to the screen. "So, an internal security risk just turned into a psychotic C.A.T.H.I.S. is loose on Earth?"

"We'll find her," replied North. "We can include the local authorities and just tell them she's a normal infantry soldier that snapped. Maybe one of them will get lucky and take her out."

"No police. No regular military. Not yet," said Dzu. "How many dead?"

"At least five. All inside the facility."

"You must contain this, Colonel. You do understand the ramifications of —"

"Don't worry. We'll find her." He paused. "In fact, I'm sure she'll come to us."

"The sister?"

"Yes."

"Then handle it. I'm activating the handler and other assets to assist."

North swallowed hard. "Do you think that's —"

"It's done. He'll be there in an hour."

"Very well —"

Dzu's screen went black.

"Shit," cursed North as he held his hand to his knee.

Chapter 6

Kayla sat across the small café table from young man in a conservative suit. She smiled as he continued their small talk. Xander Billings was perfect boyfriend material; he was a year older, cute, fun but not wild, and had a great job with the government.

"Did you see the wave about the soldier from the hospital found dead in her room this morning?" asked Xander.

"Yes…it's horrible," replied Kayla. She needed this date to get her mind off everything that had happened the night before with Cathis, and Xander's blue eyes and blonde hair was the perfect remedy…as long as he didn't want to talk about a woman's murder. "Is it okay if we talk about something else?"

"Of course," replied Xander with a smile. "I have something for you."

"A present? Now that's more like it…gimme."

Xander slid a small red felt box across the table and Kayla snatched it.

She opened the box. Inside was an ornate bracelet.

"It's beautiful," she exclaimed.

"You deserve it, K. I know we've both been working a lot lately and I wanted to give you something to remind you of me while I'm off running errands for the magistrates."

"I don't need a bracelet to remember you," replied Kayla, placing it on her wrist opposite of her communications device.

"Well, if you don't need it," replied Xander, feigning reaching for her wrist.

"But I'll keep it," she said, yanking her arm away. But she moved too fast, winching from a sore shoulder.

"Your shoulder still hurting?" asked Xander.

"A little." She looked up to see Xander's lip curled in anger. "But she didn't mean to do it. She doesn't realize how strong she is sometimes."

"Have you heard from her?"

"No." Kayla sighed. "And after last night, I don't know if I will." She felt the tears welling up again. "Every time I see her, there's less of my sister there and more of the…" She paused, not wanting to say the word *monster* aloud. "…whatever it is that *they* made her."

Xander placed his hands on hers. "I'm sorry, K. You're always upset after she visits. Maybe it's better you didn't see her when she's home?"

Kayla pulled her hand away, shooting Xander a harsh glance.

"I didn't —"

"I know what you mean," she said softly, almost a whisper. "And you're right. It does hurt sometimes. But I can't give up on her, not as long as there's any bit of Michelle left."

Xander took her hand again. "But she's given up on you. When is the last time she reached out to you without you prodding her?"

"It doesn't matter," snapped Kayla. "You don't understand what she's been through ... what drove her to become…what she is."

He took her rebuke and offered a smile. "I just don't like to see you upset. Let's talk about something else. How's the new account going at work?"

Kayla wiped her cheeks, happy to change the subject. "It's going good. Miss Kelly is really happy with my suggestions and said Mrs. Xing is interested in us designing the entire house. They want a permanent place to stay in the metro-city when they visit from Beijing."

"That's great, K."

"It is. I think Miss Kelly wants me to run the actual layout and setup." Kayla didn't notice Xander glance at his phone as she continued. "I might get to take on my own clients if this goes well. If that happens —" She paused, realizing he was reading a message.

Most people just used their wrist devices but Xander's bosses made him lug around a heavy, outmoded phone.

"Xander?"

"I'm sorry," he said. "That's great news. It's just … It's Magistrate Shay." He glanced at the phone again. "I have to —"

"Go ahead," huffed Kayla.

Xander tapped on the screen and a hologram of a middle-aged man in a suit appeared above it.

"Magistrate Shay, how can I help you?"

"I need to speak with you regarding a sensitive case," said the man gruffly.

Xander closed the hologram and placed the phone to his ear. "Yes. Of course, Magistrate." He looked toward Kayla as Shay spoke. 'I have to go…' he mouthed.

"I'll talk to you later then," she said with a sigh.

Xander stood and blew her a kiss. "I'm sorry." He turned to walk away. "Oh, not you, Magistrate."

As Xander walked away, Kayla let out a long breath, closing her eyes. As she did, a memory flashed into her consciousness:

A seventeen-year-old Kayla stepped out of the dressing room to show Michelle the dress she'd chosen for the school dance.

She'd always wanted Michelle's opinion on dresses, and since this was the first dance Kayla would attend after their mother's death, it was more important than ever.

"What do you think?" asked Kayla, slowly turning in a circle.

Michelle looked her sister over, tilting her head and placing her hand to her chin. "It's good but…"

"You don't think he'll like it?"

"He'll like it, K," replied Michelle. "But you want a dress that will destroy him."

***

"Miss Harper?"

Kayla opened her eyes to see an OE SOS officer standing over her. He was tall, with a bald head and a perfectly fitted uniform.

"Yes?"

"Ma'am. I'm Captain Burns with OE SOS. Can you come with me?"

"Why?" asked Kayla. Is Mich…Is Cathis okay?"

"You really need to come with me, Miss Harper," said Burns, offering no more.

Kayla stood defiantly. "Not until you tell me what's going on."

Burns looked around and exhaled. "There's been an accident, but we can't talk about it here.

Colonel North has ordered that you be escorted home so —"

"What's happened to my sister?"

"We can tell you in a more private location, but you should return home and pack enough to be with her for the next several days. Colonel North said it would take an hour or so to get you clearance, so you have a little time to gather your things."

"I want you to take me to her now," demanded Kayla as she began to pace back and forth.

Burns moved closer and placed his hand on her shoulder. "She's going to be okay, Miss Harper. You can pick up a few things before we take you to her…I promise she'll still be there."

"Okay. She's going to be okay" said Kayla, nodding her head to help convince herself. "Let's go."

"We have a car waiting," said Burns and Kayla quickly followed him to a nearby military hover car.

Climbing inside, she saw a second officer.

"This is Lieutenant Miles," said Burns.

"Don't worry," said Miles. "We'll get you to your sister as quick as we can."

***

Cathis scanned the area as she and Michael stood outside the door of a ground level apartment in a run-down section of the metro-city. Abandoned hover cars, even a few wheeled vehicles, were scattered along the trash-coated streets.

"This is where you're bringing me?" she asked, her mouth curled upward in disbelief.

"Just a minute," replied Michael, knocking on the door. As he waited, he looked down at her wound. "Are you sure you're okay?"

"What?" It took her a second to understand what he was asking "Oh," she replied, looking down at her stomach. "I'm fine. Nanocells are already doing their job."

"Doesn't it hurt?"

Cathis laughed. "Pain's up here," she said, poking her finger against Michael's temple. "Not here," she continued, jabbing him in the stomach.

"O…Okay," coughed Michael as her jab partially knocked the wind out of him. "I —"

The door slowly opened, drawing their attention.

A middle-aged white man with balding brown hair stuck his head through the partially open door. "Is this her?"

Michael glanced back to Cathis, still in uniform with a bullet wound in her stomach. "Who else would it be?"

"Were you followed?" asked the man.

"No," answered Cathis. "Are you Jacob?"

The man looked over Cathis and slowly opened the door.

As Cathis entered, the man stepped away from her. "Cathis is it?" he asked. "Welcome —
"

Cathis pushed past him, scanning the room for threats.

The interior of the room looked like she expected based on what she had seen outside. There was an old cloth-covered couch and a couple of over-used virtual reality chairs sitting across from a holographic TV. On the couch sat a Japanese-American woman in her mid-twenties. She was slim with multiple tattoos and shoulder length jet- black hair. She was snuggled up to a large man, a Pacific Islander with his arms covered in traditional tattoos. Most of their bodies were covered by a blanket.

"This is Mika and Hank," said Michael.

"And I'm Stiles," added the man that had opened the door.

Cathis gaze was locked on Mika and Hank. "You can tell her to go ahead and pull the gun out."

Stiles let out a sigh and gave Mika a nod.

"Fine," huffed Mika, removing the blanket to expose and old 12 gauge pump shotgun. "We don't know shit about you," said Mika to Cathis. "I mean besides the fact that you're one of the corporations' killing machines."

"Keep that gun pointed in my direction and you're gonna find out a lot more about me than you want."

Mika remained motionless.

Cathis tightened the grip on her rifle.

"Mika," said Stile. "Give it to Hank."

"Hmm," mumbled Mika before giving the gun to Hank and standing. "Robot bitch," she added in Japanese.

"At least I have an excuse," replied Cathis in perfect Japanese.

Mika let out a dismissive snort and turned to Stiles. "I'll be in my room."

"You can stay here with the rest of us," said Cathis.

"Bitch. You don't tell me —"

Cathis leveled her rifle at Hank, who'd stood with the shotgun in his hands. "And you can tell the others in the bedroom to come out too."

Stiles glanced toward Michael. "How did —"

"I mean it," interrupted Cathis as she placed the sights of her rifle on Hank's chest. "Now…or I'll fucking open up his chest."

"Just tell them to come out, Stiles," said Michael.

"Sarah, Mark, come out!" shouted Stiles. "And leave the weapons." He turned toward Hank. "You too. Put it away."

Hank reluctantly leaned the shotgun against one of the chairs and sat on the couch as Mika joined him.

Two people walked out of the bedroom. One was a heavy-set, black man with thick curly hair and the other was a tall, fit woman with olive skin and straight black hair.

"This is Thomas and Sarah," said Michael.

"Tell me again why we should trust this *thing*?" asked Mika, leaning back against Hank.

"Because that's what Jacob wants," answered Stiles.

"And where is Jacob?" asked Cathis, turning toward Michael. She stepped in close to him. "I'm done with all this bullshit."

Michael looked toward Stiles.

"This way," said Stiles, motioning toward the bedroom.

Cathis followed Stiles and Michael into the bedroom. It was cramped with clothes and other items scattered across the floor and bed.

"What's this?" said Cathis as she scanned the room. "Don't see anyone else in this shithole." Cathis was growing tired of their games. "Where the fuck is he?"

Stiles slowly opened the closet door.

"More fucking clothes!" yelled Cathis, raising her rifle toward Stiles.

"Just wait," offered Stiles, grabbing an armful of clothes from their hangers and tossing them onto the bed. He then moved a rack of shoes and a rug from the floor.

Underneath was a wooden trap door.

Stiles knelt and lifted the wooden door to reveal an armored door with a keypad lock.

"We have to keep up appearances," said Stiles as he punched in the code for the door.

Cathis brushed Stiles aside and looked down the opening.

"Your answers are down there," said Michael.

Cathis made her way down the vertical ladder, all the while keeping one hand on the rifle directed toward the dim light below.

Ten feet from the bottom, she released her grip and hit the floor, her rifle pointed toward the hallway below.

Three men stood waiting for her.

Two men, although in civilian clothing, wore tactical vests and gear and were armed with automatic rifles. Between them was a man of average height with slight Asian features and short black hair, wearing only a sidearm.

"Captain Harper," said the third man. "It's good to finally see you. I'm Jacob and we have a lot —"

"What the hell is happening?" interrupted Cathis. "And what did you people do to me?"

"Just follow me and I'll take you to a meeting with some of my lieutenants. There, we'll tell you everything." He extended his arm down the passageway. "They're just down the hall."

Cathis scoffed. "Lieutenants? You don't look like military to me."

Jacob laughed. "Not anymore. Just a figure of speech. If you're ready for answers, follow me."

Cathis followed Jacob in silence down the hallway to a plain metal door. The two guards took up a position at each side as Jacob entered with Cathis and Michael behind him.

At the far end of the room was a standard metal desk with documents spread about and two tablets resting on the surface. On the wall to the right was a row of computer screens with media reels and CAT commercials streaming across them. In the center were three people seated at an old wooden conference table, their attention focused on Cathis.

Cathis looked over the new people. To the left was a man in his mid-thirties. His body was wiry but not thin. He had a tight face and a stern look as he stared down Cathis. Unlike Jacob, Cathis had no doubt this man was, or had been, military — and not a regular.

Next to him was a slightly overweight, graying man and on the right was a blonde woman in her forties wearing a medical coat.

"Who are they?" asked Cathis.

"Silas Greene is our security lead," answered Jacob. "Frank Solas heads up our tech and surveillance, and Dr. Rachel Harding is our resident medical and genetic research specialist."

"And what is it you do, Jacob?" asked Cathis.

"I lead this section of the Restore American Democracy movement."

Cathis stepped back, positioning herself to cover those in the room and the guards at the door. "Fucking radicals!" she shouted. "I knew it."

"Wait!" pleaded Michael. "You don't understand."

"I understand enough." She shook her head. "It all makes sense now…you've planted all of this in my head."

"Of course you'd think that," said Silas.

"Because it's true," replied Cathis, moving closer to the exit.

"Please. Wait," pleaded Michael. "Just give us a moment."

"To spin more lies?"

"No," said Jacob. "We have nothing to do with the memories you are seeing other than helping you recall them."

"Lies!"

Rachel stepped toward Cathis. "Cathis —" She froze as Cathis swung her rifle toward her. "I — just tell me this…do these images feel like they're made up?" She moved slightly closer. "Or are they real?"

"It can't be real…not all of it." She grunted in frustration. "If you're with RAD, then you're all traitors!"

"Traitor?" laughed Silas. "Against who?" Unafraid, his eyes shot daggers at her. "The corporations? The corrupt senators? The heads of CAT? They're the ones that have betrayed the people."

"Easy, Silas," warned Jacob. "She needs time to adjust to the reality of things."

"Reality?" huffed Cathis. "The reality is that you have taken an OE SOS officer and you've done…something to…"

Jacob raised his hands to calm her. "I know it's a lot to take in. I also know that all of your training and experience is telling you to turn us in."

"Or kill us," added Silas.

Cathis turned toward Silas. "You said it."

"That's what you're built for, right?" said Silas.

"Silas, that's enough!" ordered Jacob.

Jacob turned toward Cathis. "I know you could kill us all if you wanted. Hell, you've probably already worked it out in your mind how to do it."

She had.

"Yes. You could do it," continued Jacob. "But would it matter? OE SOS and CAT are after you, too. You're one of their most expensive and dangerous weapons and they've lost control of you. They'll put you down the first chance they get."

Cathis stood silent.

"Maybe they should at that," said Silas.

She centered her sights on Silas, but as she did another memory ripped into her consciousness. "No!" she shouted as she stumbled but quickly regained her footing.

"We can help you understand what you're seeing," said Jacob. "I promise."

Grunting as the memory faded, she slowly lowered her rifle.

"Should she have a weapon right now?" asked Frank.

"It doesn't matter," replied Rachel. "She could kill us without it," she added, slowly moving toward Cathis. "You really did it, Michael. You got her out."

"Well," replied Michael. "To be honest, she got herself out and I just kinda followed her."

Rachael moved even closer, but something told Cathis she was not a threat. Soon she was standing directly in front of Cathis. "So you remember? Then the software worked. I —" She stopped, looking down at Cathis' wound. "Oh."

Rachel moved her hands toward Cathis' shirt but Cathis quickly brushed them away.

"I just want to check you out," said Rachel. She made a motion to indicate to Cathis she was going to lift her shirt.

"Go ahead," replied Cathis.

"Nanocells?" asked Rachel.

"Yes."

"Self-clotting?"

"Yes."

Rachel looked back up toward Cathis. "Does it hurt?"

"The firing rate of nerve cells in the area of the injury is reduced to limit distractions, but once you're comfortable with pain, it doesn't really matter anyway."

"Fascinating," said Rachel as she pulled Cathis' shirt back over her abdomen.

"I'm glad you're fascinated," replied Cathis, "but someone needs to tell me what the fuck is going on."

"Yes," replied Jacob. "Everyone sit."

Cathis watched as everyone took a seat at the table.

"You too," said Jacob.

"I'll stand," she replied.

"Very well." Jacob took a breath. "You, and those like you, are tools used as part of Consolidated Armaments Technologies' plan to destroy what is left of our democracy."

Cathis' skin grew hot. "You did…whatever you've done to me…so you can bring me here and spout radical propaganda?" She again took a defensive stance. "This has to be some kind of RAD deception?"

"You know," replied Rachel.

Cathis took a deep breath. As horrible as they were, the flashbacks felt more real and visceral than any memory she'd ever had except…the one from the night that changed everything.

She eased her stance.

Jacob raised his hand slightly to calm her but continued. "And it's not just Mars or Titan or some random space station…" Jacob leaned forward, his eyes locked on hers. "They're using you on Earth."

"No!" shot back Cathis, shaking her head. "That's impossible. It's against the Accords —"

Silas laughed, drawing a cold glance from Cathis.

"You've seen it," said Jacob. "In your flashbacks…the memories they've repressed."

"No! There's no —"

Another memory hit her.

***

Cathis was back at the farm house. The American flag was burning. She looked down at the dead. They were wearing American insignia and U.S. Army uniforms.

"No!" she screamed.

***

"No!"

As Cathis' scream faded, she lowered herself into one of the chairs at the conference table. "It can't be true. That's not what we…what I do."

"That's what you all do," spat Silas. "They just conveniently wipe those little tidbits of savagery against your own people from your memory every time you do it."

"But I wouldn't." She looked up toward the group, tears in her eyes. "I'd never kill one of our own —"

"You have to understand," said Rachel, "CAT has thought this out very well. It's not hard to manipulate the scenarios, Captain. Any one act, no matter how horrible, can often be motivated by subterfuge and justified by a lie. Then, under the guise of a mission download, they go into your memories and tweak them ever-so-slightly, removing or modifying the parts they don't want you to know."

"They tell you the targets are traitors or criminals," said Frank. "And since you don't remember the other times you've done it, you believe it's a single mission worth breaking the Accords."

"Just like a good robot," added Silas.

Cathis' gaze shot to Silas. "What is your fucking problem? Why do you hate me so much?"

"You don't have time for me to tell you how many different ways I hate your kind."

"How 'bout you try to pick one?" grumbled Cathis.

"Fine." Silas leaned toward her. "One mission you've conveniently forgotten was the one where you attacked a protection detail for the Senatorial candidate, Rebecca Sanchez."

"No," replied Cathis. "She died in a transport accident —"

Silas laughed. "That's what the corporate-controlled news told everyone. You and your team hit her convoy and killed her."

"No. That's impossible."

Silas slammed his fist into the table. "I was there!"

***

Major Silas Greene sat in the third of four black-tinted armored hover craft as they sped down a small mountain road in the darkness.

As he looked across the seat toward Los Angeles Councilwoman Rebecca Sanchez and her assistant, he could see the assistant was anxious.

"Another thirty minutes and we'll be at the rendezvous point and turn you over to LAPD special services," said Silas.

"Is all of this really necessary?" asked Sanchez's assistant.

"You're in good hands, ma'am," replied Silas with a smile.

"I just don't understand why we need the military to transport us to LA," replied the assistant.

"The DOJ and DOD established a liaison group so we could provide protection across jurisdictions for your kind. All I know is we were assigned to get you to LA, and since Mrs. Sanchez was designated as an HVT —"

"HVT?" asked the assistant.

"High Value Target," said Sanchez. "It just means I've caused some problems for the cartels and a few businessmen in China."

"So, we're…targets?" asked the assistant.

"The good guys usually are, but don't worry. There isn't a team on Earth that's better than my —"

A nearby explosion rocked the hover car and it came to a stop. Another explosion, this one closer, rattled the car.

Silas checked the status of the convoy on his tactical tablet as gunfire erupted outside. "Shit!" He activated the comms device on his tactical vest. "Gator One, this is Raptor One. We're under fire. Car One and Four out of action. Request —"

Bullets began to ricochet off the car, cracking the bulletproof glass.

Silas turned toward the driver. "We need to find cover. Drive through the wreckage."

"Yes —"

The assistant lunged forward, driving a knife into the driver's neck then pivoted toward Sanchez, who had fallen onto the floor of the car. Silas slammed his boot into the assistant's torso, knocking her back into the seat, but she recovered and landed a knee against his ribs.

He let out a grunt but grabbed the assistant's hand, still holding the knife, and with a growl drove it into the woman's neck. Shoving the assistant's body onto the floor, he turned toward Sanchez, who was curled into a ball in the corner of the car.

Silas kicked the door open and leapt onto the ground. He quickly leveled his weapon at two armed men dressed in black tactical gear who rushing toward him.

He opened fire and they fell backwards. "We have to go," he said, extending his arm to her.

"Let's go!" he shouted toward Sanchez as he took her hand to pull her from the car.

Before he could react, one of the men he had shot stood and crashed into him, knocking him to the ground. As he fell, he pulled his pistol from his vest.

The attacker straddled him and raised his gun first, but Silas fired two rounds into his chest and one into the helmet that covered his entire face. The round penetrated the helmet, but the man, although dazed, didn't fall.

"Fuck!" he cursed as he fired three more rounds into the helmet, finally causing the attacker to fall.

He rose to his feet and saw two of his men firing into the rocks above the road as they stood behind the hover car, protecting two of Sanchez's staff.

Silas continued his story, his gaze fixed on Cathis. Cathis' expression was blank, save a steady stream of tears rolling down her cheeks, as if she were seeing the story replay in her head as he told it.

"We were DELTA and this team took us apart like we were nothing. A burst of machine gun fire tore into my two men and the staffers…ripped them to shreds."

Silas paused.

"And their leader…"

Cathis mouth was agape as she relived the carnage from her vantage.

***

Cathis' sights landed on a major and the target.

A burst from her rifle knocked them both to the ground, but the major had pulled the target to the left at the last second so the rounds hit her shoulder and his leg instead of being kill shots.

"Fuck," cursed Cathis into her helmet. "I've got eyes on target. Clear out the rest of them."

Cathis leapt from behind her covered position and rushed toward the major and the target.

The major leveled his pistol and fired. The round hit Cathis' shoulder, twisting her body slightly but she didn't lose her stride.

She was on him in another step and kicked the pistol from his hand.

She drove her fist toward the major's head, but he blocked her punch and swung his boot toward her head. The impact knocked her helmet to the ground but she was unfazed.

Cathis grabbed the major and slammed him against the wrecked hover car. He let out a loud grunt but grabbed a knife from his vest and drove it toward her torso.

Cathis caught the major's hand with her own and with the other, threw him back against the car and onto the ground.

Drawing her pistol as she turned, Cathis looked down at the target, Rebecca Sanchez.

"Please," begged Sanchez. "I —"

Cathis sent a round through her forehead and turned back toward the major, who had pulled himself to his feet and was rushing toward the edge of the road.

She fired and the major's body twisted and fell, disappearing over the steep hill.

Cathis walked to the edge and down toward the river several stories below.

He was gone.

***

Cathis' tear-filled eyes were staring down at the table. She watched the drops fall onto the wooden surface. "I remember," she confessed. "They told us she was working with the Medina cartel and that your team were mercenaries."

Her stomach tightened and the room began to spin. Unable to hold back, she leapt from the table and ran to a nearby receptacle where she emptied the contents of her stomach.

Panting, she rolled onto her behind and sat by the trash can with her head in her hands.

"I didn't know…" she mumbled. "I didn't know."

"Three days later," added Frank, "wreckage of a hospitality craft was found washed ashore and DNA matching Sanchez and her staff was found."

"And why would a candidate for Senate take a vacation in the middle of a contentious campaign?" asked Silas.

Cathis looked up from the floor to Silas. "Why didn't you report it?"

Silas grunted. "I came to on the bank of the river at the bottom of the ravine with two of your bullets in me. I slowly made my way back to the convoy after your team left then reported the attack and called for medical support…they reported an ETA of one minute." Silas shook his head in frustration. "There was no way they had medical evac one minute out, so I thought something was wrong and moved further back but reported that I was at the convoy." Silas took a deep breath. "Thirty seconds later, three thermo missiles hit the remnants of the convoy…they wanted to make sure there were no survivors."

"After that," added Jacob, "Silas realized he couldn't go back and found his way to us. His story confirmed our beliefs that OE SOS had been carrying out CAT sponsored attacks on their political and financial rivals."

Cathis slowly stood, feeling the eyes of everyone on the room resting on her. Shame and regret washed over her. She was unable to speak.

"So tell me," asked Silas, his words dripping with hate. "Is it the killing that you regret … or the fact that they took your memories so you couldn't reminisce?"

"Fuck you."

Silas leapt to his feet, throwing his chair across the room. "Fuck me? You killed good men that day."

"I didn't know!" She doubled over, heaving as her stomach wretched.

"I believe you," said Jacob, placing a reassuring hand on her shoulder. "But now that you know, you can help right all of those wrongs."

Cathis stood erect. "How?"

"By sharing your memories," said Rachel. "We have the CAT process for the procedure. We can access your memories again. Except now you'll have full recall."

"We can see the missions CAT and OE SOS want to keep secret," said Michael. "And bring them to their knees."

"We'll take those images," added Jacob, "and upload them to the unsecured net. We will let the people see what our current leaders are allowing CAT and OE SOS to do here on Earth."

Cathis took a deep breath. The thought of even more nightmares coming to light sent a chill down her spine. *'And for what end purpose?'* she thought as she worked through the repercussions of such an act. "And what good will that do?" she asked.

"Then the people will know," said Jacob. "They'll see the truth and hopefully enough of them will stand up and —"

"And do what?" asked Cathis. "An uprising of any size will be the final excuse CAT and OE SOS will need to take control of the military. They'll be ruthless in putting down any resistance…it will mean civil war."

"Then let war come," said Silas.

"That's easy for you to say," said Michael. "You're a ghost to them. For some of us, that blood being spilled won't just be ours but that of our families as well…you know what CAT will do to stay in power."

A jolt shot down Cathis' spine. "Kayla."

"Who?" asked Silas.

"My sister," said Cathis, as fear and anger began to build up inside her.

"If you have a sister, then they probably already have her," said Silas.

"We can send people to get her now," said Jacob. "Silas can lead —"

"No. I'm going," said Cathis.

"But we need you to stay," said Rachel. "We have to get the download started. It —"

"You're not getting shit from me until my sister is safe."

"Yes," said Jacob. "And Silas —"

"I said I'll get her," repeated Cathis.

"We can handle it," said Silas.

"Like you did with the convoy?" snapped Cathis. She turned back to Jacob. "When Kayla is safe, you'll get what you want."

"Fine," said Jacob quickly, hoping to prevent Silas' response. "But you need to get out of that uniform."

"We can get you some clothes right now," offered Rachel.

Jacob glanced toward Silas, then back to Cathis.

"Fine," grunted Silas.

"Fine," said Cathis.

"I'll go with her," replied Michael.

***

Cathis and Michael exited the bunker via an alternate location and walked toward a nearby hover car.

Michael made his way to the driver's side and activated the door.

"I'll drive," she said.

"But shouldn't —"

She grabbed his arm, stopping him from opening the door. "I said I'll —"

Cathis doubled over, falling against the car.

"Another flashback?" asked Michael.

But Cathis didn't respond. She had retreated too far into her mind.

He knelt down next to her as she pressed her hands against her face, her body spasming.

"No! No! No! No!" she panted.

Michael could tell this flashback was even worse than the first one she had in the CAT facility. "Cathis?"

Her convulsions slowed and she sat with her head toward the ground, breathing heavily.

"Cathis?" Michael placed his hand on her shoulder. "Are you okay?"

She slowly raised her head, letting out a pathetic, sad laugh. "No. I'm not," she looked up toward the sky and took a heavy breath.

"What was it?"

Her gaze returned to his.

"I was a new lieutenant with only a few missions completed. Our objective was a shitty little farming settlement. The environment barely supported the RSR families living there … no tactical or strategic value whatsoever." She let out a weak, disgusted chuckle. "But that didn't matter. They were just in the wrong place and OE SOS wanted to keep RSR out of the sector so they sent us in. Regular troops would have been more than enough…but they wanted to make a statement. Hell, their only defense was a small militia detachment…fucking farmers with old weapons."

"You were just —"

"No," interrupted Cathis. "You don't understand." She exhaled. "We walked right over them like paper targets on a training course." Her expression shifted from one of frustration to a blank, far-off gaze. "We were mopping up in less than an hour. Corporal Smith, First Sergeant Greeves, and I entered a small bunker…we would've just tossed a grenade in the room and been done with it, but OE SOS brass wanted us to take their leader so we could video him confessing their claim on the settlement as illegal. So we went in…" She stopped, slamming the back of her head against the hover car. "We went in…I moved right, Smith left, and Greeves took the center. We cleared the room and came together at the opposite side." Another heavy, painful breath escaped her. "That's where they were."

"Who?"

"Two fucking girls," grunted Cathis. "One twelve, maybe thirteen, and the other seven or eight."

He placed his hand on her shoulder again. "You don't have to —"

"Yes. I do," said Cathis, shrugging his hand away. "I knew what we were supposed to do…but I couldn't. I couldn't do it," she said, now sobbing.

"That's good," replied Michael.

"No!" shouted Cathis. "Greeves waited for the order and when I didn't give it, he turned toward me and asked what was wrong. I told him there was no reason to kill them. He started talking about following orders, things got heated, and then Smith got involved." She closed her eyes, fighting off a wave of convulsions. "We got distracted and…" She shook her head. "Fucking rookie mistake…the older girl grabbed a piece-of-shit shotgun hidden nearby that we'd failed to clear. She pointed it toward Smith."

"What happen —"

"So we shot her. Greeves and I tore her fucking body apart while her little sister let out…"

She stopped, trying to push the screams from her mind. "…she let out a scream like I'd never heard before or since."

"I'm sorry," said Michael. "Horrible things happen out there, I know."

"Shut up," groaned Cathis. "We stood there looking at this little girl as she tried to hold what was left of her dead sister." She looked back into

Michael's eyes. "Do you know what two bursts from an M-43 rifle will do to a little girl's body?"

The pain in her gaze was undeniable as she continued. "I told Greeves we weren't going to kill the other girl." Another forced, painful breath. "Then he said it…he laughed and called me a cold motherfucker because there was no way we'd take her with us, so we'd just be leaving her there to die in the blackness of space…alone with her dead sister."

"What did you do?"

"I put a round through her head," replied Cathis, her voice broken and weak.

Michael leaned back, away from her. After a second, he recovered. "That's a lot to have wiped and then forced back —"

"They didn't fucking wipe it!" groaned Cathis.

"What?"

"I've never forgot that day…I just eventually stopped caring," she sobbed. "I shot that little girl and just learned to be okay with it because it was better than the alternative. We left nothing but death in our wake…and death was often better than anything else we offered."

"But CAT and —"

"CAT or OE SOS didn't do that! I did!" she shouted. "I wanted so bad to be strong that I stopped caring about the weak…"

Her body began to shake and she began to slam her head against the car repetitively until Michael could see a dent form in the door.

"I can't do this," she panted, grabbing the pistol from her waist belt.

"No!" shouted Michael, pushing with both hands against her wrist as Cathis moved the pistol toward her temple.

Michael pressed hard, using his entire body to slow the motion of her arm. But he couldn't stop her. "What about Kayla?" he blurted.

He felt her arm slack and quickly took the pistol from her.

He'd never seen her look as vulnerable as she did there, leaning against the car, lost in her own past of violence and death.

She was in no condition to move, let alone save her sister. He sat silently as Cathis slowly regained her composure.

"Are you going to be okay?" he asked. "We can go back and get Silas?"

"No," replied Cathis. "I have to…"

He put his hand to her cheek and she let him guide her gaze toward him.

"What did you want to do more than anything when you volunteered to become a C.A.T.H.I.S.?"

She huffed but didn't answer.

"Tell me?" he asked, trying to help her focus.

"I wanted to become strong so I would never be afraid again."

In the short time he'd known her, Michael had realized what really drove Cathis.

"But even after that, after all the power you have, there's still one thing that scares you…"

"Keeping Kayla safe," she replied, her expression shifting from shame to determination.

"Good," said Michael. "Then use what they did to you…what you've become…to do that very thing." He stood, extending a hand to her. "Are you ready to do that?"

She took his hand and slowly rose to her feet.

"Then let's go get your sister," said Michael.

Chapter 7

Michael drove cautiously down the dark, quiet street leading to Kayla's house. As he did, Cathis scanned through the files contained on a tablet Michael had provided to learn details about Kayla's neighborhood. She analyzed everything. Entrance and exit paths, nearby buildings, known metro-city security camera locations.

"Stop here," she said suddenly.

Michael obliged. "Why here? We're still five blocks from your sisters."

Cathis activated a tab and a 3-D model of the area illuminated above the flat tablet screen.

"The city cameras start in two blocks, so they'll probably have one or two roving teams covering the perimeter a block or so out."

Cathis studied the hologram, her brow furrowed in thought.

"So what's the plan?" asked Michael.

"This is Kayla's building…five stories tall. They'll have two two-man teams with rifles on top of the building." She moved her finger toward the tallest structure. "An over-watch team will be here…about five hundred yards…again two men. They'll have two more teams of two roaming the ground level and two at each entrance."

"How do you know —" He stopped. If anyone would know OE SOS tactics, it would be her.

"Kayla's on the third floor, so they'll probably have a few on the stairway and officers will be in the apartment with her." She paused. "They'll have two tactical teams ready to go…probably here and here…far enough not to be easily spotted but close enough to respond quickly. We'll need to be in and out before they are activated."

"And how are we going to do that?"

"They'll be on a reporting timeline for comms," answered Cathis. "Typical is fifteen minutes, but we'll assume ten to be safe."

"Safe…you're talking about taking on twenty OE SOS troops."

She looked toward him and scoffed. "They're regulars, and they're stationed on Earth, so it shouldn't be too difficult. And it's more like thirty including the tactical teams, but we don't want them engaging…then the numbers start becoming an issue."

"Sure, twenty is much better."

"Yes," continued Cathis, not catching his sarcasm.

"And how are you going to get past them and then back out."

Cathis smiled.

***

Cathis gripped the drain pipe of the building tight with one hand as she balanced her foot against the exterior wall. Glancing at the ground eight stories below, she saw one of the patrols move past her and marked their location.

"Eagle three reporting. All clear," came the voice of one of the two soldiers on the top of the building.

It was time.

Cathis pivoted her body and kicked upward, then pulled hard with her arms, shooting her body onto the top of the roof.

The sniper recoiled in surprise, but she landed a boot to his head, knocking him unconscious. The spotter reached for his communicator but she drove her fist into his throat. Grabbing the man's shirt, she torqued her body and tossed him off the roof with one hand.

Twenty-seconds.

Cathis picked up the rifle and swung it toward the roof of Kayla's building. Her sights rested on the team on the opposite side of the structure.

She glanced at the range and wind speed indicator and slowly exhaled.

Cathis pulled the trigger, shifted the sights slightly, and pulled the trigger again.

Peering through the scope, she saw both rounds impact the targets.

Next she shifted to the team closer to her.

The spotter has repositioned himself directly beside the sniper.

"Two birds," she whispered before taking in a breath and exhaling.

She fired and both men slumped over, dead.

Standing, she moved to her right and found the two roving soldiers.

Two rapid, well-placed shots had them dead on the ground.

One minute, ten seconds.

Cathis dropped the rifle. She removed the spool of rope from her torso, attached it to a nearby stanchion, and tossed the other end over the ledge. Looking over the edge, she could see Michael pulling the dead soldiers into the brush below.

Wrapping the rope into place around her, she stepped off the side of the building.

When she hit the ground, she quickly scanned the area before moving toward her objective.

One minute, forty-five seconds.

She slowed her pace to a walk and turned the corner toward the back entrance of Kayla's building.

Two soldiers came into view at the door.

She continued forward, her head lowered toward the ground.

"Sorry, ma'am," said one of the soldiers as she made her way up the short set of steps. "Official —"

Cathis drove a knife under the first soldier's chin toward the back of his neck as she simultaneously pushed the second soldier's head backwards. With a grunt, she twisted and pulled the knife from the first soldier's body, tearing a gash through the left side of his neck and slashed the throat of the second.

As they fell, she stepped into the building.
Two minutes, five seconds.

***

Kayla shoved one last shirt into her bag and exited her bedroom to approach the waiting OE SOS officers.

"Okay. Take me to her," said Kayla, fighting to control her anxiety.

"We'll need to wait just a bit longer," said Burns.

Kayla moved toward the door. "But you said we could go as soon as —"

The second officer grabbed her arm. "We're gonna stay right here for a while."

"Let me go!" demanded Kayla, trying to free herself from Miles' grasp.

"I said sit!" grunted Miles as he tossed Kayla onto the couch.

Burns stood over her. "We're all just gonna get nice and cozy here for a while."

"Where's Cathis?"

"That's what we're hoping you're gonna help us with."

"What are you talking about?" asked Kayla.

Burns smiled. "Seems like big 'sis has lost her shit … so we're gonna just sit tight and wait for word she's been neutralized or for her to try to contact her little sister."

"I don't understand. I thought she —"

"You don't need to understand, little girl," said Miles. "You just need to —"

A thud outside of the apartment drew everyone's attention.

Both men turn toward the door, drawing their pistols. Burns turned on his communications device as Miles took up a defensive position to the right of the door.

"What's happening?" asked Kayla, her heart pounding.

"Shut up," ordered Miles.

Burns crept toward the door and activated the entry camera. The holographic screen illuminated, showing a dead soldier at the entrance.

Then a flash.

Burns raised his pistol as the door exploded open, sending him flying across the room.

***

Cathis stepped through the door.

Ignoring Kayla's scream, she grabbed the pistol out Miles' hand before he could fire, cupped his head, and slammed it against the wall. She spun around, drew a knife from her belt and drove it into the back of his neck. Letting Miles' body slump to the ground, she turned back to Burns.

Burns raised his weapon, but Cathis kicked it away.

He pushed himself off the floor, trying to activate his communicator, but she grabbed his arm, torqued her body, and sent him flying across the room. He hit the floor hard, struggling to take in air. Cathis was on him instantly, lifting him off the ground and slamming him against the wall. She held him pinned there, his feet dangling.

"One tac team or two?"

"Screw you."

Cathis grunted in anger and with her other hand, grabbed the man's right wrist and snapped it like a twig.

"How many?" she asked over his cries.

"It doesn't matter. We'll send as many as it takes to end you." His mouth curled in a sadistic smile as he glanced toward Kayla. "Then we'll take care of your little sister —"

Cathis drove her fist into the man's throat, crushing his larynx.

As he fell to his knees, she slammed his face into the floor with a crunch of bones and a splattering of blood.

She raised her boot above his head and brought it down with a growl, breaking his neck.

Three minutes.

Cathis turned to Kayla. "We have to go."

Kayla didn't answer. She stood with her arms wrapped around her body, shivering.

"Kayla!"

Kayla let her body fell back onto the couch. "You just … those were OE SOS officers. Why are —"

Cathis knelt next to Kayla, placing her hand to Kayla's cheek. The unexpected contact from Cathis caused Kayla's gaze to shoot upward from the floor to her sister's eyes.

"Cathis?"

"Don't call me that anymore," she said. "I've found out that OE SOS and CAT…" Tears began to well up in her eyes. "They've…I've been killing people on Earth."

Kayla leaned away. "What? No."

"And because I know, they're after me." She ran her hand over Kayla's face. "And they'll hurt you to get me."

"Cathis, what —"

"No, not anymore," she said, leaning her forehead against Kayla's."

"Michelle?"

Michelle felt Kayla's hands against her face.

"I'm so sorry," wept Michelle. "But we have to leave now," she said, standing.

Kayla stood, but her gaze went toward the dead men on the floor.

"You killed them —"

"They were going to hurt you."

"I don't —"

Four minutes.

"We really have to go, Kayla."

Kayla remained still. "I don't understand what's happening."

Four minutes, ten seconds.

"Kayla!"

Kayla's body jerked, startled.

Michelle exhaled heavily. "Do you trust me?" A jolt of fear shot through her when she realized she didn't know what Kayla would say.

"I —"

"Do you trust me to keep you safe?"

"Yes. Of course," said Kayla.

"Then come with me. Please."

Michelle extended her arm and Kayla took her hand.

Four minutes, thirty-five seconds.

Michelle exited the apartment with Kayla behind her. As she scanned the stairwell, a young man rushed up the steps.

She centered the barrel on his chest as he saw her, his eyes wide with shock.

"No!" shouted Kayla. "He's…with me."

"Who is this?" she asked, the rifle still pointed at Xander.

"Xander. He's…he's my friend."

"What's happening, K? Are you okay?" asked Xander.

Five minutes.

"We don't have time for this, Kayla."

She stood like a statue. "I don't —"

Michelle let out a groan of frustration and turned back toward Xander. "Get out of the way or I'll move you."

Although she could see the fear painted on his face, Xander stood defiantly. "Where are you taking her? I'm not leaving …" He paused, realizing the barrel of Michelle's rifle was still aimed at him. "I am not leaving until I know she's okay and where she's going."

Michelle saw Michael moving up the stairs behind Xander.

"What's taking so long?" He paused, seeing Xander. "Who's this?"

Five minutes, thirty seconds.

"A complication," answered Michelle.

"What the hell is happening?" asked Xander.

Michael looked at the time on his wrist device. "Five minutes and —"

"I know," interrupted Michelle, her frustration growing. Cathis would have put a bullet in him and moved on, but Michelle hesitated.

She glanced toward Kayla. Her sister's eyes were pleading.

"Then we go. All of us."

"Fine," huffed Michael.

"I'm not going anywhere until —"

"You can walk with us or I'm going to knock you out and carry you," said Michelle.

Xander's blank stare was his answer.

"Then move," ordered Michelle, as she moved down the stairs with the others following.

Six minutes.

Hopefully they could make it back to the hover car in time.

***

As they sped down the hover way, Michael, Michelle, Kayla, and Xander sat in silence.

Michelle looked across the seat at Kayla and Xander. Kayla was still visibly shaken, holding tight onto Xander's arm.

Michelle's attention focused on Xander's wrist, and his wrist communicator. "Shit," she cursed as she pulled the device from Xander's wrist and tossed it from the car.

"Hey! What are you doing?" huffed Xander.

"You can't have anything they can track us with," said Michelle. She looked toward Kayla. "You need to get rid of yours, too."

Kayla complied, throwing her device out of the window.

"What is that?" asked Michelle.

"That's just a bracelet," said Xander.

"It was a gift," added Kayla. "It's not a communicator."

"Fine," replied Michelle.

"Oh, Xander. Your phone."

"A phone?" asked Michelle. "Why do you have a phone?"

"I..."

"He needs it for his job," said Kayla. "He works for the magistrates."

"Yes," said Xander, pulling the phone from his pocket. "In case the magistrates —"

"You work for the government?" said Michael, glancing back toward them as he drove. Shaking his head, he turned his attention back to driving. "Fucking great."

Michelle took the phone, snapped it in two, and threw it from the window.

"Do you know how crazy this is?" asked Xander. "This doesn't make any sense."

"That's why there's dead men at Kayla's apartment, because it's all so ridiculous."

Xander leaned back in his seat. "So what happens now that you've made me a fugitive?"

"Better a fugitive than a corpse," offered Michael as he continued to drive.

***

"What the fuck happened?" yelled North toward the screen.

"I don't know, Colonel," replied an OE SOS lieutenant standing outside of Kayla's apartment. "We didn't receive a call for my team and there was no indication of a problem until teams started missing their communications check-ins."

"How many dead?" grumbled North. "And has the scene been contained?"

"Twelve dead. We've secured the area, no one's going in or out."

"Except your primary fucking objective!" shouted North, slamming his hand into the desk. "She waltzed right in and out under your fucking noses?"

"How long was the comms reporting cycle?" came voice from behind North.

North spun around to see First Sergeant Greeves, in tactical gear, standing behind him.

"It would be you," said North, turning back toward the lieutenant on the screen. "Well, how long?"

"We increased from fifteen to —"

"Ten minutes," interrupted Greeves, letting a knowing huff escape his mouth. "She probably did all that damage in five."

The lieutenant didn't have an answer.

"Finish sanitizing the scene," ordered North before closing the screen and turning back toward Greeves. "You're probably loving every minute of this, aren't you?"

Greeves smiled. "You squirming?… a little." His expression tightened. "But regardless of the insane amount of money CAT is paying me, this has become a real shit-show."

"Whatever…we'll find her —"

"You better. And soon."

"We will."

"Not without me," said Greeves.

"CAT and OE SOS have a lot of resources looking for her, Greeves," replied North.

"I know about the other assets you've got in play, Colonel," said Greeves. "But they'll fail."

North guffawed. "And why is that?"

"You really don't understand what you guys made with this one, do you?"

"She's no different than any of the other C.A.T.H.I.S.," said North. "They all the same genetic enhancements, same interface hardware, software —"

"But very different cores," said Greeves.

"Nonsense."

"Sure, she's got basically the same mods as the others," replied Greeves. "But in her case, you modified a fucking main battle tank and not your mother's hover car."

"They all had excellent —"

"Yeah, I know. They're all strong, intelligent, and emotionally broken to some degree." He paused, his mouth curled in a smile as he acknowledged how special Michelle Harper had really been. "But our girl…college gymnast, played Mozart by ear, and a doctoral student in theoretical physics." He laughed. "Hell, even without the tactical interface mods, she would have been a general someday."

"And that's why we recruited her, if you remember."

"And she said no," replied Greeves. "She wasn't broken like the others. Sure, her parents had died but she was strong and confident…didn't blame anyone for it. So, when you offered her the chance to be a solider, she told you no."

"But she eventually changed her mind," said North, repositioning himself in his chair, uncomfortable with where he knew the conversation was going. "After appropriate leverage was applied."

Greeves laughed aloud. "Leverage? Give me a fucking break. She said no and it pissed off the heads of CAT so they…and you —"

"You don't have to fucking tell me what happened."

"But you're gonna hear it because it's why I'm going to have to eventually clean up your fucking mess," replied Greeves as he walked toward North, looking down at him. "You used her psychological profile and figured out exactly what needed to happen to break her."

"Fuck you," grumbled North. "You know as well as I do that when the CAT heads decide they want something —"

"And now they're reaping what they sowed. They took a brilliant, incredible athlete with a natural ability for asymmetrical thinking and problem solving and turned her into a killing machine."

North scoffed at Greeves, turning away from him. "They're all killing machines."

Greeves grabbed North's collar, turning him back toward his gaze.

"I've seen her literally rip a human apart." He leaned in close. "What do you think she's going to do when she figures out — and she *will* figure it out — that CAT paid those guys to break her so she would join your program?"

North stared back at him blankly.

"What do you think she's going to do to you?"

"We'll get her first," replied North, trying to convince himself as he contemplated Greeves' question.

"For your sake, I hope so," said Greeves. "But the sooner you realize that I'm the only one that will be able to stop her, the better off you will be."

"And why is that?"

"I know you'll have their locations soon, and you'll send in the other assets, but she'll kill them all because you think she can be defeated head-on."

"And just how would you defeat her, Greeves?"

"The only thing that beautiful death machine cares about more than vengeance is her sister," answered Greeves. "And when I make her feel like she's helpless to protect her precious Kayla, I'll do more damage than those three assholes CAT paid to rape her ever could have."

Chapter 8

Jacob opened the door to the conference room.

"Who's this?" he asked, seeing Xander.

"This…was unavoidable," said Michael.

"Fine," replied Jacob. "Come in."

Cathis and Michael led Kayla and Xander into the room.

In addition to Jacob, Silas, Frank, and Rachel, two armed guards were inside.

As they entered, Silas grabbed Xander.

"Hey!" shouted Xander.

Kayla reached for him. "Xander!"

"Who is this?" asked Silas. "The deal was just the sister."

A guard began to frisk Xander, as a second placed his hands around Kayla's torso.

Michelle grabbed the guard's hand and twisted his wrist, driving him to the floor. "She's clean," she said, her focus on Silas.

"Both of them are," added Michael.

With a nod from Silas, the guards stepped back to the edge of the room.

"It'll just take a few minutes to get you ready for download," said Rachel. "If you'll follow me to the treatment room?"

"Download?" Kayla turned toward Michelle.

"They're gonna go into my head and get proof of everything CAT and OE SOS has done."

"Then what?" asked Kayla.

"Thanks to Frank," answered Jacob, "we'll use what's in Cathis' memories —"

"Don't call me that anymore," said Michelle. "I don't want to…call me Michelle."

Jacob smiled. "Of course. Frank will hack into the network and upload Michelle's memories on all unsecured channels. They'll shut it down pretty quickly, but it should be long enough to light the spark. People will see what CAT and OE SOS have done, with support of our government —"

"How do you know the government is involved?" asked Xander.

"They'll be plenty of proof when we play the files," said Frank.

Xander responded by walking over to the wall by the guards.

Kayla turned toward Michelle. "Is this the right thing to do?"

"Come with me," said Michelle as she took Kayla's hand and led her to a small couch away from the others. Kayla sat and Michelle knelt next to her, gripping her sister's hand tightly — but not too tight — as she spoke. "Honestly, I don't know." She exhaled heavily. "I thought what I was doing was necessary to keep our people…to keep *you* safe." She closed her eyes and the tears that had formed rolled down her cheeks. "But I let them turn me into a monster."

"Michelle," huffed Kayla, tears now filling her eyes. "You're not —"

"I just didn't want to be afraid anymore and they used that to —" She paused. "I even took their name, thinking it would destroy the weak girl I was…" She forced out a heavy breath, tears clouding her vision. "…but now it's the name of a murderer."

Kayla, her tears now flowing, pressed her hands against Michelle's cheeks. "What have they done to you?"

Kayla stared into the eyes of the sister she had known before.

"I'm sorry," wailed Michelle as they embraced.

The flash of lights and the blaring of an alarm broke them out of their embrace.

"What is it?" asked Jacob.

Silas placed his hand to an earpiece. "Fucking OE SOS. They just took out our team at the apartment and are cutting through the entrance to the tunnel."

"How did they find us?" asked Frank.

Silas pointed to Kayla. "Check her again."

Michelle stepped in front of Kayla. "Don't fucking touch her."

"Look," grumbled Silas. "It has to be one of them."

"We need to surrender or they'll kill us all!" pleaded Xander. "I didn't ask for this."

"Shut up!" ordered Silas. "Check them both."

A guard stepped toward Kayla but Michelle drew the pistol from her belt. "I said no."

The guard leveled his weapon.

"Wait!" shouted Kayla, stepping in front of Michelle. "Just let them check us."

"You've brought me here to die!" shouted Xander.

"Not one more word from you," said Silas. "Now check them both."

The guards moved forward and began to run detectors over Xander and Kayla's bodies.

As the device reached Kayla's wrist it let out an electronic beep.

"What is that?" asked Silas.

"It's just a present from Xander," she answered.

Silas grabbed the sensor. "It's a fucking beacon."

The room turned toward Xander.

"I'm sorry, K," said Xander.

"Xander?" asked Kayla.

Xander grabbed the pistol from the guard's vest and fired a round into his torso.

Michelle dove toward Kayla, knocking her to the ground and covering her body as gunfire erupted.

Soon Kayla's screams replaced the gunfire and Michelle looked up to see both guards down and Silas, with his pistol in hand, standing over Xander's body.

"Rachel!" yelled Jacob.

Michelle shifted her gaze and saw Rachel, sitting upright, leaning against the wall.

"Son of a bitch!" cursed Silas.

Kayla, pushing herself off the ground, stared at the bracelet on her wrist for a second before pulling it off and tossing it across the room.

Silas activated his communicator as Michelle and Jacob rushed to Rachel. "Activate evac plan bravo."

Michelle looked down at Rachel. Her white shirt was quickly turning red as blood oozed from a chest wound. Rachel soon began to gasp for air.

"It's okay," said Jacob. "We'll get you out of here."

"No," coughed Rachel. "It's too …" She grabbed Jacob's arm. "Get to the Peninsula outpost. You can do everything from there."

Jacob placed his hand to her cheek. "Okay, when we get you there —"

"I'm not going," she replied, turning toward Michelle. "You…" As smile formed on Rachel's mouth.

She was gone.

Muffled gunshots told them the tunnel had been breached.

"We need to —" Silas paused, listening to his earpiece. "Fuck! They have a C.A.T.H.I.S. with them."

Michelle felt the eyes of everyone in the room turn toward her.

"I'll throw the rest of our teams at them," Silas said to Jacob. "Maybe we —"

"No," interrupted Michelle. "Your teams need to cover the retreat. I'll deal with the front door. You get everyone out."

"Fine," replied Silas. "I'm coming with you."

"No. I need you to make sure my sister is safe."

"You can't take the risk," said Frank. If anything happened to you —"

"That won't matter if they kill everyone here." Michelle turned back to Silas. "You get Kayla to safety."

Silas acknowledged the trust Michelle was placing in him with a nod.

She now shifted her gaze to Jacob. "And after I take care of them, we'll be able to get the word out."

"I guess I really don't have a choice, do I?"

"You don't," replied Michelle.

"No, Michelle," said Kayla, running to her sister. "I don't want to leave you."

Michelle leaned down, placing her forehead against her sister's. "It's okay, K. I'm the only one that can stop them."

Stepping away from her embrace with Kayla, Michelle picked up a rifle that had belonged to one of the guards. "You're not losing me again. I promise." Checking the rounds, she turned toward Silas. "Go."

"Michael and two guards will give you cover and Michael can get you to the outpost," said Silas. "Here," he added, handing her an earpiece for communications.

"Just keep her safe," replied Michelle.

As the others made their escape, Michelle turned to Michael and the two guards. "Just cover my flanks and back. Fast and violent," she said. "That's what this needs to be." She paused. "And if you see another like me, keep putting rounds in it until you're out of ammo."

***

As the gunfire intensified, Michelle, Michael, and the two guards stacked up against the wall by a corner.

A security guard ran past them, only to fall as rounds ripped into his back.

Suddenly silence fell over the passageway ahead of them.

"They'll be coming," warned Michelle. "Fast and violent."

Michelle pivoted and turned into the passageway and fired at two OE SOS soldiers. As they fell, she was already moving past them.

Another OE SOS soldier stepped into view from behind a storage cabinet, holding a combat shotgun.

Michelle rolled forward as he fired, buckshot impacting the wall behind her. Letting her rifle swing by its strap, she rose to her knees and pushed upward. She grabbed the shotgun with one hand as the man fired, blowing a fist-size hole in the ceiling.

Dropping the shotgun , she drove her boot into the man's knee. As he cried out in pain, she wrapped her hands around the back of his head and drove his face into her knee with a crunch.

Looking at her ammo count on the rifle, she dropped it to the floor and picked up the shotgun. She knelt, quickly taking the dead man's vest containing additional ammunition.

"Where are the others?" asked Michael.

"They probably split up into three teams. This one here, a team for corridor B, and a team to find the power station."

"How did you know about the other corridors?" asked Michael. "You've only been down this one."

"I saw the prints for a few seconds the first time I met Jacob. Poor OPSEC leaving them out, by the way."

"And the C.A.T.H.I.S.?"

"Holding back. Waiting to see which team finds me…or doesn't respond," said Michelle as she reloaded the shotgun. She looked down at the dead OE SOS men. "So they'll be coming."

The comms crackled in Michelle's ear. "Contact!" shouted Silas over the sound of gunfire.

"What's happening?" asked Michelle.

"There's a team in the utility exit. We should be able to get —"

"Cover!" shouted Michelle, spinning behind the cabinet as bullets filled the hallway.

The two guards crumpled under the fire and Michael fell back against the wall by Michelle with a wound to his abdomen.

Michelle fired two shots down the passageway and turned to Michael. "That's the C.A.T.H.I.S.," she said. "Are you okay?"

"All up here," panted Michael, pointing to his head. "Right?"

"Right."

"Cathis!" came a booming male voice echoing down the hallway. "You've been very bad."

"Johnson?"

"Yep," replied the voice. "You've caused enough trouble. Now drop your weapon and come out."

"You've been lied to, Johnson. CAT has —"

Another volley of rounds flew down the passageway.

"They said you'd lost it," said Johnson. "Now come out or I'm coming in."

"I'm not surrendering."

"Didn't think you would."

Michelle turned back toward Michael. "If he gets past me, put every round you have into him."

"You don't have to tell me," huffed Michael.

Michelle tossed the shotgun into the passageway.

"Let's do this right, Johnson," yelled Michelle. "Let's see who has the bigger dick."

A rifle came sliding down the floor next to the shotgun.

"Let's go," came Johnson's answer.

Michelle stepped into the passageway.

A tall, lanky man stepped into Michelle's view and slowly removed his helmet. He was in his early thirties with olive skin and a tight haircut.

Michelle smiled. "You're way off mission, Johnson. You should be putting a bullet in my brain right now."

Johnson replied with a smirk. "My mission is to kill you. They weren't specific as to the details."

The two warriors slowly walked toward each other.

"I guess you know I never really liked you," said Johnson. "Hell, I volunteered for this one."

"You've been in the service long enough to know better than volunteering," replied Michelle. "You done flirting?"

With a growl, Johnson rushed forward and Michelle raced to meet him.

Michelle blocked Johnson's first swing, but she felt a snap and pain registered as he landed a boot to her ribcage. Grunting, she landed a blow to his jaw that staggered, but did not drop, him.

Stepping in for a kick, Michelle fell backwards as Johnson landed an open hand to her chest. Michelle's back impacted the wall, but she sprung forward and knocked him to the ground with a kick from her right leg.

Johnson rolled and jumped back up to a defensive position.

Michelle leapt toward him, and in a series of blows and counters, they moved back and forth from one wall to the next.

Johnson pivoted and swung his leg toward her, but Michelle caught his lower leg. Wrapping her arm around his chest, she swept his leg and drove him into the floor.

Michelle stood over him, waiting for him to rise.

"You're holding back," said Johnson.

"Just wanted to give you a —"

Johnson burst forward, picking Michelle off the floor and slamming her against the wall. Holding her in place, he leaned in. "Stalling to let your sister and those traitors get away? It doesn't matter. All that matters is that you die."

Michelle landed a blow to his jaw with her elbow, but he recovered and slammed his forehead into hers, knocking her back against the wall.

"And they're not going anywhere," he smiled. "Chan is waiting for them."

Michelle's face tightened. There were two C.A.T.H.I.S. in play. She had to get to her sister.

Michelle pushed Johnson's arm from her neck and pulled it to his side.

"I am stalling," she said through gritted teeth. "Because I'm better than you."

She pressed her back against the wall and with a grunt kicked Johnson in the chest, sending him flying into the opposite wall.

He quickly stood but Michelle was on him, pulling a knife from her vest as she closed in.

Johnson swung toward her head but she blocked the punch.

As she diverted Johnson's arm, she dropped low and drove the knife into his thigh, hitting the femoral artery. She twisted it free only to sink the blade into his liver before yanking it out with another twist and driving the knife into his armpit. Pulling the knife free again, she flipped it in the air to change her grip and sank it with a growl into his neck near the collarbone.

Johnson let out a groan and sent Michelle flying against the opposite wall.

"Fucking bitch," he cursed, spitting blood from his mouth.

Johnson, the knife still in his neck, reached for his pistol.

But Michelle was too quick.

As Johnson leveled the pistol, she fired three blasts from the shotgun and stepped toward him, the last step ending with the barrel pressed against his forehead.

She turned to Michael. "Can you walk?"

Michael responded with a nod, unable to speak as he was absorbing the violence he'd just seen.

"That's what it takes to kill one of us," said Michelle. "Now let's get to the others."

***

Silas fired a burst and an OE SOS soldier fell twenty yards away as bullets ricocheted around the large pump foundation he was using for cover.

"We need to get to the docks," said Jacob. "This is taking too long."

"Once team two works their way around their flank, we should be able to —" Silas paused, taking a report from Michelle over the communicator. "Damn it!"

"What is it?" asked Jacob.

"There's another C.A.T.H.I.S. at our end," replied Silas, looking toward Frank and Kayla. "Shit," he cursed, taking a deep breath. "You guys need to make a run for the docks…now. I'll take a team forward and press them. Hopefully, we can distract them long enough for you to get away."

"What if there's more at the docks?" asked Frank.

"You go with them," interjected one of Silas' men, Zach. "We'll keep them busy here until you're at the hover boat. Then we'll make for the alternate evac location."

Silas paused, struggling with his decision. His men would be killed, he was sure of it. But they knew the risks.

"Okay." Silas turned to Kayla, Jacob, and Frank. "When I move, you stay close and don't stop."

Silas placed his hand on Zach's shoulder. "Good luck, brother."

Zach give him a nod of understanding and

activated his communicator. "James, Rodriquez, and Mann. On my mark, move forward to that generator. Conner and Horn, you follow me."

Zach gave one more glance toward Silas. "Make it worth it."

***

Zach crawled across the pump room, blood from multiple wounds leaving a trail behind him as he attempted to find cover.

A single set of footsteps echoed across the room.

Rolling onto his back, Zach saw a wiry figure in black standing over him. From the outline, he could tell it was a large, powerful female, her face obscured by a helmet that covered her entire head.

He raised a pistol only to have it kicked away.

The soldier reached down with one hand and picked him off the floor, pressing him against a large piece of machinery.

"I'm not telling you anything," spat Zach.

The solider pulled a knife from her vest with her free hand and placed it to Zach's neck.

***

"No matter, traitor," said Chan as she squeezed the Zach's neck. "Your friends won't get very far. And when *he* catches up with them, they'll wish it had been me."

Chan slid the blade across the man's neck as blood sprayed over her uniform.

Dropping the body, Chan spun to her right, bringing her rifle to the ready just as a blast from a shotgun sent her toppling backwards.

***

Michelle moved forward, the shotgun pressed to her shoulder as she scanned the room.

Stopping at Zach's body, she saw a blood trail leading away toward rows of electrical distribution panels. "Damn it," she mouthed.

Crouching low, she moved along the edge of the panels, following the blood until she came to a corner. Taking a breath, she spun into the opening.

Nothing. No Chan. No blood.

"Shit," grumbled Michelle, noticing blood several feet up on the panel. She turned around.

Both Michelle and Chan opened fire.

A round tore into Michelle's leg as buckshot ripped into Chan's shoulder and arm.

Michelle fell backwards but raised her weapon and fired again. Her round hit Chan's helmet, knocking her backwards while Chan's rounds impacted the panel above Michelle's head.

Chan leapt forward as Michelle rose.

Michelle attempted to fire again, but Chan directed the muzzle away, the round blowing a hole in the panel opposite them in a flash of electrical sparks and acrid smoke.

Michelle moved her right hand from her gun and grabbed the receiver of Chan's pistol as she fired, but the round plowed through the flesh of Michelle's arm. Next, Chan spun to her side and slammed her knee into Michelle's forehead, crashing her head into the panel behind her.

Dazed, Michelle loosened the hold on Chan's arm and Chan fired another round into Michelle's wounded leg. Letting out a grunt, Michelle shoved Chan backwards.

Chan hit the opposite panel and swung her pistol toward Michelle, but before she could fire, Michelle grabbed the shotgun, shoved it underneath Chan's helmet at the chin, and fired.

Pushing herself off the floor, Michelle started to assess her wounds but stopped. It didn't matter, she needed to get to Kayla.

Chapter 9

Silas scanned the dimly lit dock. Several shipping crates and containers were scattered across the pier with a few hover boats magnetically docked in place.

"Let's go," whispered Silas, creeping toward the nearest container with Jacob, Frank, and Kayla behind him. From his vantage behind the crates, he saw their boat.

"That's it," he said, pointing toward a modest looking vessel about fifty feet away. "Quietly."

Silas scanned the pier as they moved, moving his rifle from one potential threat to the next.

Soon they were at the boat.

Silas stopped at the gangway leading to the boat, motioning for the others to move. "Just head down and the pilot will get ready," he said as the three reached him.

Jacob nodded and started down the gangway. At the first platform, he stopped, looking back toward Silas.

Jacob's eyes were wide and his face was pale.

"Jacob," said Silas moving past Jacob, "what is —"

Hitting the first platform, Silas saw the pilot's body on the deck just inside the cabin. "Damn it! Everyone —"

A shot rang out and Frank fell, disappearing into the dark water below.

Silas pulled Kayla past him to the first level as rounds began to impact around him.

"Where's Frank?" asked Jacob.

"Get back in the —"

Jacob's head snapped backwards and he fell into the cabin.

"Fuck!" cursed Silas as Kayla let out a scream.

Turning toward Kayla, he shoved her down the ladder into the cabin and jumped down behind her.

"Just stay hidden," said Silas. "And don't come out unless I tell you."

"But —"

Silas put his hands to his mouth, warning her to be quiet as footsteps could be heard moving down the gangway above.

Motioning for Kayla to hide behind a table in the cabin, Silas pointed his rifle at the entrance above.

A shadow flashed at the entrance and Silas fired a burst from his rifle.

His volley was answered by a shower of bullets tearing into the cabin.

"Stay down!" shouted Silas.

Silas fired again as he moved toward the opening.

Jutting his upper body through the opening, he saw a man in black tactical gear with a wound to his shoulder rising back up.

Both men fired.

Silas' body jerked to the left, dropping his rifle, as a round hit his torso.

But one of his rounds found its mark, hitting his opponent's left arm.

Both men grabbed for their pistols.

***

Kayla heard the flurry of gunfire and looked up to see Silas' body tumble down the ladder onto the deck.

Her heart pounded. She struggled to control her breathing as a shadow slowly moved across the wall by the entrance before a boot became visible in the ladder.

With nowhere to run, she ducked back behind the couch and stared blankly at his shadow cast against the wall. The man slowly made his way into the cabin.

"Here kitty, kitty," said the man.

She remained silent.

A gunshot sounded and she let out an involuntary gasp.

"Gotcha," said the man.

Kayla curled her body into a ball, trying to make herself as small as she could.

"Hello there."

She saw a boot next her. Falling backwards, she looked up to see a man in his thirties with close-cut dark hair and a thick beard. His mouth curled in a maniacal smile.

His shirt was stained with blood and his left hand was mangled, but he seemed unfazed.

She kicked at him but he brushed her legs aside and grabbed her by the hair, jerking her to her feet.

"Come on, sweetie," he said. "Me and you are gonna wait for big sis out on the dock."

***

Michelle emerged from the water, gripping the gunwale of the boat. Sliding the shotgun from her shoulder, she took a breath and in one motion leapt onto the deck.

Scanning the area, she moved toward the cabin, leaving a bloody trail of water behind her.

At the entrance to the cabin, she swung the shotgun toward the opening.

At the bottom was Silas' body. Looking past Silas, she saw the bodies of Jacob and another man.

Shifting her focus, she saw a blood trail leaving the boat and moving up the gangway. As she followed the trail, she glanced down to see Frank's body floating in the water. Moving off the gangway onto the pier, she moved toward a row of container boxes.

Michelle stopped as two people emerged from the shadows.

"Kayla, are you —" She froze, seeing Greeves behind her, holding a knife to her face.

Michelle dropped the shotgun and drew her pistol.

"No. Not you too," gasped Michelle.

Greeves positioned himself carefully behind Kayla to prevent Michelle from having a clean shot.

"You've caused a lot of trouble for some powerful people, Cathis," he said.

"Don't call me that. That name is based on a lies."

"Whatever," said Greeves with a chuckle. "Looks like the other murder-bots did a number on you."

"You should see them," replied Michelle.

"Figured they wouldn't get the job done," replied Greeves. "The suits thought they'd take care of this but they've never really seen you in action. I knew it'd have to be me."

Kayla tried to pull away but Greeves pulled her close. She winced as he tightened his hold.

"Let her go," said Michelle.

"Don't think so."

"You don't understand," said Michelle. "All of this is a lie. CAT and OE SOS has been using us —" She stopped, her jaw tightening. "You know, don't you?"

"Of course I do," replied Greeves.

"Then why?"

"The same reason I've done everything. Money. Lots of money."

"Fucking asshole." Michelle's head began to spin but she kept the pistol pointing in the direction of Greeves, waiting for him to give her a clear shot. "All those missions …"

"CAT needed to keep an eye on their investments so each one of you got one of us."

As the betrayal sank in deeper, she started to lower her pistol but quickly brought it back into position as Greeves continued.

"We were assigned to put down any of their little death machines that went rogue. And honey, you've gone rogue."

"So you're fine with killing our own people?"

"Of course. Especially since they pay us extra for those missions. They'd leave the regular OE SOS troops behind and it would just the C.A.T.H.I.S. and their handlers…but of course you wouldn't remember any of that." He paused. "Or I guess you do know now…and that's why you need to be put down."

Michelle gritted her teeth. "Let her go. I won't say it again."

Michelle's heart skipped as Greeves pressed the blade against Kayla's cheek, causing a small trickle of blood to flow.

"I don't think so," said Greeves. "Instead, how 'bout you put that pistol to your temple and blow your brains out…or I'll slice her up right in front of you."

Michelle paused. She knew what Greeves was capable of doing.

"Michelle. No. Don't —"

"Shhh," said Greeves, placing his left hand to Kayla's cheek, smearing his own blood across her face.

Michelle looked down the barrel of her pistol, desperately looking for a clear shot.

"All that strength and speed, that tactical fucking computer in her head," said Greeves, "and you can't do a single thing to stop me from taking the one thing in the world you actually care about."

"Don't fucking do it, Greeves," said Michelle. But this time it came out more as a plea than a demand.

"Big bad predator is just gonna watch me carve up her little sister," taunted Greeves. Because at your core, you're still that weak little bitch…"

"Fuck you," grunted Michelle.

"Just as helpless as that night when those men took you —"

"What?" Michelle's heart pounded and her stomach tightened. How did he know?

"CAT always get what it wants, Harper," said Greeves. "They wanted you then…" He paused. "…and just like that night, there's nothing you can do to stop it."

Rage exploded from her very core. "They did…" She lowered her pistol slightly as the realization of the true path to her becoming what she was sunk it. "No. No." She let out an audible growl, raising her pistol again.

Greeves gave Kayla's hair a tug, causing her to grunt from the pain. "All that rage and still nothing you can do without me killing her first."

Michelle struggled to find an opening for her pistol while her entire being was coming undone.

"I'm not fucking joking," grumbled Greeves. "Do it or I'll gut her."

Michelle stood motionless. She knew he would do it. Even she wasn't fast enough. "If you do it, I'll fucking rip you apart," she warned, knowing all she could do was offer him a painful death for taking his sister's life.

"Probably," replied Greeves. "But she'll still be dead. And then you'll truly have nothing. Be nothing…but what they made you."

Kayla let out scream as Greeves slid the blade across her cheek, slicing it open.

"Do it!" he boomed.

Michelle stepped toward him but stopped as he placed the blade against her throat.

"Last chance. Now be a good robot and do what you're told."

Michelle's heart pounded. She couldn't see a scenario where she could take out Greeves before he killed Kayla.

"If you do it, I'll make sure your little sis gets a head start." He laughed. "I'm pretty fucked up myself; she might just get away."

Michelle looked toward Kayla and smiled. "I love you."

"No!" shouted Kayla.

Michelle slowly placed the pistol to her temple. "It's going to be okay."

"No!" pleaded Kayla.

Michelle closed her eyes. The image of her and Kayla playing as children ran through her mind as a smile formed on her face.

The crack of a gunshot echoed across the pier.

Michelle's eyes shot open.

She saw Michael step out from behind a container, pointing a smoking gun toward Greeves.

Greeves dropped the knife and staggered away from Kayla as blood poured from a bullet wound to his neck. His face was vacant as he grabbed at the wound, blood oozing through his his fingers.

Michelle raised her pistol toward Greeves and let out a scream as she opened fire and moved toward him. Six rounds tore into his body before she stopped over his corpse, firing two more rounds into his forehead.

The emotions and her injuries beginning to take their toll, Michelle dropped the pistol and fell to her knees.

Kayla rushed toward her.

Michelle looked up to see her sister's bloody check. "You're hurt."

"I'm okay," replied Kayla. "We're both okay."

Kayla looked back toward Michael. "We need to get her to a doctor."

"We all need a doctor," replied Michael. "But I can get us there."

Epilogue

Colonel North sat alone in the study of his spacious apartment. He took a slow drink from his scotch as he watched the news report of a RAD attack on a CAT weapons storage facility.

He glanced back to confirm the OE SOS guard was posted just outside of his study.

An icon illuminated at the top of his screen. Colonel North opened the video file.

At first there was static, but then a clear picture from Cathis' point of view appeared as she led the attack on Rebecca Sanchez's convoy. North watched intently as he saw the view from the barrel of Cathis' weapon shooting Sanchez.

"Damn it," he cursed.

The screen went to static and then clear again as a young woman with a scar across her face appeared. She spoke:

"What you have just seen is video evidence of the murder of Senatorial candidate Rebecca

Sanchez by OE SOS soldiers, led by C.A.T.H.I.S. troops. This blatant attack was carried out on American soil at the direction of Consolidated Armaments Technologies and with full knowledge of key members of our civilian and military leadership. This is just a glimpse of the atrocities carried out by CAT to further their plan to destroy the last vestiges of democracy and replace it with oligarchic rule. We have sat by long enough while our freedoms have been eroded. This video should be a wake-up call to all Americans. Stop believing the lies. Stand up and fight against the tyranny of CAT and an increasingly corrupt government."

The camera tightened on the woman's face.

"My name is Kayla. I allowed myself to be a willing victim of this tyranny for years…but no more. From this day forward I pledge, along with my brothers and sisters in the Restore American Democracy movement, to take back my country…by whatever means necessary."

North poured the rest of the scotch in his glass into his mouth and swallowed hard.

Another icon illuminated and he opened it.

"Mr. Dzu —"

"This has gotten out of control," interrupted Dzu. "I'm assuming you have seen the video?"

"I have."

"It was wide-released ten minutes after an explosion at one of our research facilities."

"I am aware," said North. "This is just a minor setback."

"Minor setback?" In the two months since you allowed her to escape, we've had eight facilities attacked and lost over one hundred men just in the Seattle-Tacoma metro-city alone…and now this video."

"We will have the unsecured net shutdown until we can wipe the video … we'll just say it was a possible cyber intrusion by the Caliphate or the Restored Soviet Republic. These extremists —"

"Colonel," interrupted Dzu. "So, your answer is that we must expend even more resources to…" Dzu paused, leaning toward the screen. "What is that?"

North saw a shadow in the screen and turned.

***

Michelle slammed North's head against the desk and drove her knife deep into neck at the base of his skull.

As blood pooled on the table, she looked into the screen at a shocked Chinese man in a suit.

"You! What have you done?"

Michelle sneered at Dzu. "He thought he was untouchable. I touched him."

"You will not get away with this. You are nothing but a rabid dog. We will hunt you down and kill you."

"You can try …" Michelle moved closer to the screen, looking at the call information. "Xang Dzu from Beijing," she replied. Her face tightened. "But you didn't make us into dogs. You made us lions." She paused. "And you must remember, when you're hunting a lion … it's hunting you too."

Dzu involuntarily leaned back from his screen.

"Be seeing *you* soon," said Michelle as she turned off the screen.